CREDO

FUNDAMENTAL CHRISTIAN BELIEFS

THOMAS S. KEPLER

WILDSIDE PRESS

CREDO

Reprinted from *motive*, October, 1944, through May, 1945.
Copyright, 1944, 1945, by the Board of Education of
The Methodist Church

D

SET UP, PRINTED, AND BOUND BY THE
PARTHENON PRESS AT NASHVILLE, TEN-
NESSEE, UNITED STATES OF AMERICA

To

MY STUDENTS

1930–1945

FOREWORD

THE METHODIST STUDENT MOVEMENT SEEKS TO PRACTICE WHAT may be called the democratic-educational method. The attempt is made to utilize the contributions of individuals and groups and, through the discipline of the Christian fellowship, mold their offerings for maximum usefulness. Each student group is a laboratory in democracy for the creation, evaluation, and practical application of Christian ideals.

In the operation of this process and with natural organizational growth the Methodist Student Movement has now become a conscious cohesive force. Sponsored by The Methodist Church, it has developed into a significant church student movement. Its main emphases to date have been democratic group practice, churchmanship, and Christian social action.

There has been a growing concern among some that a movement may develop with an inadequate intellectual and philosophical and religious undergirding. It courts the danger of shallow activism. This would be especially unfortunate for a voluntary religious group of college students in the setting of higher education.

One year ago the executive committee of the National Student Commission and other student leaders, constituting a planning committee, met to formulate plans for the Third National Student Conference, which it is hoped can be held during the holiday season of 1945-46.

The process and the tendencies were discussed. There was spontaneous undergraduate expression of the fact that there

5

is great danger that voluntary religious student groups may overstress methods, program, and projects. In so doing, it is actually possible to miss the real meaning of contemporary historical events and fail to have the kind of religion that is at once deep, sound, and constructive. Therefore the students, seemingly speaking for a great mass of their fellow students, and desiring that the forthcoming national conference be a natural part of the ongoing program process of their movement, urged that the following be done (the language is ours):

1. Make an analysis of what is happening in our contemporary society. Make it with a thoroughness and with such scientific soundness that we may realistically come face to face with the crisis of our time.
2. If Christianity has an answer to give to the crisis, tell us what that answer is. What *are* the essentials of the Christian faith?
3. We will gladly give our lives through the Church. Tell us more about the Church. What is the Church? How has the Church functioned in history? What is the Church saying and doing today?

In accordance with this process these three books are being published: Dr. Paul E. Johnson's condensation of Dr. Pitirim A. Sorokin's *The Crisis of Our Age* analyzes the crisis. Dr. Thomas S. Kepler's *Credo* outlines briefly the answer of Christian faith. And Dr. William R. Cannon's book *The Christian Church interprets the Church.*

We happily commend these three books to college students everywhere who ought to be interested in the issues discussed.

H. D. BOLLINGER
H. C. BROWN
H. A. EHRENSPERGER

July 31, 1945

6

AUTHOR'S NOTE

THE SCENE IS A GARDEN IN CARTHAGE, NORTH AFRICA; IT IS THE middle of the third century A.D.; a middle-aged man, Cyprian by name, is writing to his friend Donatus. This is what he says:

This seems a cheerful world, Donatus, when I view it from this fair garden under the shadow of these vines. But if I climbed some great mountain and looked out over the wide lands you know very well what I would see. Brigands on the high roads, pirates on the seas, in the ampitheatres men murdered to please applauding crowds, under all roofs misery and selfishness. It is really a bad world, Donatus, an incredibly bad world. Yet in the midst of it I have found a quiet and holy people. They have discovered a joy which is a thousand times better than any pleasure of this sinful life. They are despised and persecuted but they care not. They have overcome the world. These people, Donatus, are the Christians—and I am one of them.

Seventeen centuries have elapsed since Cyprian wrote these words to Donatus. The problems of living have become more complex, for a machine age and a global war seem to make "brigands on the high roads" and "pirates on the seas" rather miniature evils; yet the Christian today believes that he has a way to encounter twentieth-century problems as vitally as did Cyprian in the third century. Christianity has not become outmoded; as a way of living it has remained perennially fresh. Jesus' insights, when properly interpreted, have shown the Christian "the way, and the truth, and the life" for every century; certainly this is true today for many people.

7

CREDO—FUNDAMENTAL CHRISTIAN BELIEFS

The eight sections of a *credo* portrayed in this book attempt to give a graphic "feel" regarding the vital aspects of Christianity for the contemporary man. They attempt to circumscribe the ideas at the heart of modern Christian thinking and living. While I take full responsibility for the manner in which miscellaneous ideas have been synthesized into my own *credo*, I realize also the great debt owed to many individuals—especially scholars in religious philosophy and the New Testament —for the stimulation they have given. From a grateful heart I thank them. I also extend appreciation to the magazine *motive* for allowing this material, which formerly appeared in its pages, to be here reprinted in book form.

THOMAS S. KEPLER

Lawrence College
July 28, 1945

CONTENTS

I BELIEVE IN MAN

In "THE GREEN PASTURES" NOAH MAKES A KEEN GLANCE INTO human nature when he says, "I ain' very much, but I'se all I got." With "all I got" each of us asks with deep sincerity, "What am I? And especially what am I through Christian spectacles?" He asks this because he is not only aware of the mystery of himself but also conscious of the problem he confronts in trying to make "all I got" into something of significance and worth. Recently when 270 students on an American campus were given a questionnaire, it was found that 90 per cent were suffering from complex mental frustrations. When the Harvard class of 1911 was questioned twenty-five years after graduation, it was found that one eighth of its members were financially dependent on others, and that one fourth were disappointed with their careers.[1] As a person faces these disturbing figures, he thoughtfully queries, "What *is* man?" Emil Brunner expresses the value of every person's asking himself this question: "The most powerful of all spiritual forces is man's view of himself, the way in which he understands his nature and his destiny; indeed it is the one force which determines all the others which influence human life. For in the last resort all that man thinks and wills springs out of what he thinks and wills about himself, about human life and its meaning and its purpose."[2]

[1] John R. Tunis, *Was College Worth While?* (New York: Harcourt, Brace & Co., 1936).
[2] *The Christian Understanding of Man* (Oxford Conference report; Chicago: Willett, Clark & Co., 1938), p. 146.

11

CREDO—FUNDAMENTAL CHRISTIAN BELIEFS

1. *Most of us can begin with a feeling of self-certainty; at least we do exist!* We can say with Descartes, *Cogito, ergo sum* ("I think, therefore I am"). To this admonition the Christian theist can add, "What is man, that THOU art mindful of him?" But the statement and the query are but the beginning of the quest as to what man is. Man wants to know first of all how he came into existence. The Christian fathers were content with one of two ways to explain the origin of man: (1) he was especially created by fiat as explained in the Genesis creation story, the result of God's labor on the sixth day; or (2), accepting Plotinus' view, man effulged from the One (God) as the One overflowed into the Nous (the world soul) and other souls like ourselves. Such views may satisfy modern man that God is the designer and creator of man, but such explanations do not give the *manner* of creation which pleases the contemporary thinker. The modern man accepts the descriptive facts of emergent evolution, viewing man as emerging hundreds of millions of years from less perfected life upon this planet. He sees God as the author of the process of creation and man as the end result. As he understands evolution as a theory explaining *how* and not *why* man's gradual development, he "need not believe that men are descended from the monkey, but from God, who has been immanent in all life, slowly developing from the monad to the moral person, from the single cell to man." [3] He sees that "the real dignity of man consists not in his origin, but in what he is and in what he may become."

2. *Man is an earth-bound creature; he does belong to the "good earth"; he is a citizen of the natural world, where at least 100,000 years he can be securely labeled as "man."* Chemically he is made up of acids, salts, proteins, fats, and water; he possesses carbon, hydrogen, nitrogen, and oxygen combined within him in intricate fashion so that he may retain his physical structure for "threescore years and ten" or even

[3] Sherwood Eddy, *New Challenges to Faith* (New York: George H. Doran Co., 1926), p. 35.

12

one hundred years—or for but a few hours. Yet it is not this physical structure which really makes man; the physical structure is only his substructure. With similar physical structures some have achieved goals when young; others have continued to follow their creative urge when old. Bryant wrote "Thanatopsis" when he was eighteen; Hume wrote his *Treatise of Human Nature* when he was a student in college; Newton discovered the law of gravitation and the binomial theorem when he was twenty-four; Michelangelo was a master of sculpturing when he was twenty. Yet others have kept the creative urge alive until almost death: Franklin at eighty-four was the leader of the Constitutional Convention in Philadelphia; Gladstone at eighty-five was the world's leading statesman; and

> Cato learned Greek at eighty; Sophocles
> Wrote his grand Oedipus, and Simonides
> Bore off the prize of verse from his compeers,
> When each had numbered more than fourscore years. . . .
> Chaucer, at Woodstock with the nightingales,
> At sixty wrote the Canterbury Tales;
> Goethe at Weimar, toiling to the last,
> Completed Faust when eighty years were past.[4]

3. *Man is certainly something more than a sum total of physical substances!* The biologist adds that man is an organism containing a life process which adapts itself to its stimuli and reproduces itself. The self is the result of the union of two single cells, which become an organism composed of millions of interrelating cells. The organic health affects man's metabolism, and glandular processes further affect the total reaction man may have toward the complexities of life. Yet it is not man's organic nature alone that makes him *man;* animals and plants are also organic. But a plant as an organism can reach its maturity in a few weeks; animals as organisms are able to attain their development in a few months; man as

[4] H. W. Longfellow, "Morituri Salutamus."

13

an organism takes years before he achieves his growth. When he finally attains his biological growth, he finds himself not only a citizen of the present who reacts to stimuli of his environment. As such a person he learns to *control* his environment; even more he envisions ideals for himself in the future, and glances back at history, where he feels the past in such a way that he is better able to interpret the future for his own existence. Man is a biological organism, but he possesses something which other "earthborn" organisms do not have.

As Arthur Compton perceives life on this planet from the angle of the physical and biological sciences, he concludes: "It [is] difficult to escape the conclusion that our world is controlled by a supreme Intelligence, which directs evolution according to some great plan. We could, in fact, see the whole great drama of evolution moving toward the making of persons with free intelligence capable of glimpsing God's purpose in nature and of sharing that purpose. . . . Our survey of the physical universe indicated that mankind is very possibly nature's best achievement in this direction." [5] With such an attitude toward man as a creature in the process of emergent evolution the Christian agrees. But what further can be said about man from the Christian angle depends upon the school of Christian thought to which the interpreter belongs.

4. *There are three main schools of Christian interpretation:* (1) *the left-wing school of scientific humanists* see man as the end result of emergent evolution; (2) *the right-wing school of neosupernaturalists and traditional supernaturalists* view man as God's creation, but so "fallen" that he has lost his normal relationship to God; and (3) *the theistic schools* envisage man as belonging organically to the subhuman level as part of the naturalistic process, but also related normally to the immanent Spirit of God as the spiritual life of the universe.

This first school of thought views man as a mere bodily organism who reacts to the stimuli of the natural world (the

.⁵ A. H. Compton, *The Freedom of Man* (New Haven: Yale University Press, 1935), pp. 139-40.

14

only level of reality); man's mind is the result of his neurophysiological reaction to environment; Jesus as an ideal man has shown us how we too may "discover" the *process* in nature so perfectly found by Jesus. In such a pattern of thought man is determined wholly by biological and social forces; he lacks creative freedom. Men "have each other"; and if they will but emulate Jesus in their living, the Kingdom of God will arrive in an evolutionary manner. Paradoxically enough, the coming of the Kingdom depends entirely upon men, and men are but a part of the level of nature. This school of scientific Christian humanists has but a small number of members, found mainly among left-wing Unitarians and unchurched "Christians."

The schools of supernaturalists savor of European pessimism in their view of man as a totally fallen creature, but their numbers are scattered throughout the United States in conservative church groups. The stimulus for the neosupernaturalists is located in Augustine, Calvin, Kierkegaard, Barth, and men of like temper. To these thinkers man does have the use of free will as he lives in the natural world: he can choose his profession, his political party, his ethical way of living. But he cannot choose God, because as a rational-feeling creature he is estranged from God because of the fall of man in the Garden of Paradise. Hence God must choose the man whom he wishes to save. Man is thus saved by faith, but faith is not something which man himself can create; it is the gift of God to man, mainly because God possesses grace. Therefore man has no free will when it comes to choosing salvation; he is predestined to salvation, since God chooses whom he will. Jesus Christ becomes for the neosupernaturalists a figure of greatness merely because he was completely obedient to God's will. They believe that Jesus as a man of great ideals or fine character matters little for any of us, because such a person was a part of the natural world. We call Jesus Christ "Lord" only because he has shown us how we might become completely obedient to God so that God's grace may give us faith for salvation.

These two schools which view man so differently are good "correctives" of each other. Neosupernaturalism "corrects" sci-

15

entific humanism of its homocentric view of religion where
humanity becomes the god whom men worship; scientific
humanism "corrects" neosupernaturalism of its total pessimism
regarding man and its overspeculative manner of theological
thinking. In between these two radical schools lies Christian
theism, which gives a pattern of thought that shows what many
believe to be the "true portrait" of man in relation to his
universe.

The theists believe that "reality is man writ large"; man is
the *key* to his universe qualitatively. Alfred N. Whitehead has
expressed this idea: The self "repeats in microcosm what the
universe is in macrocosm." [*] This means that the spirit of man
is to his physical body as the Spirit in the universe is to the
phenomena of nature: each is an organism, one small and one
large; within the large organism, the universe, all the small
organisms live and interrelate themselves to God and to one
another. As God is the life of the universe, each man has a life
which integrates his body; each life is intimately related to
God's cosmic life; and each man is thus "spiritually" related
to every other man. Jesus as man's ideal belongs organically to
the universe as we all do; it is his *degree* of relationship which
causes his difference from us. Each of us, because of the misuse
of freedom, is in a microcosmic manner (as a "little world")
a distorted impression of the macrocosm (God); Jesus, on the
other hand, is one who held such harmony with God (the Life
of the Universe) that God's eternal values could be clearly
reflected through him—thus the basis for the Incarnation. To
develop the spirit of Jesus Christ in ourselves brings to us a
feeling of real unity with God, which is the final purpose of the
Christian man. It is the manner by which we become "sons
of God."

5. *The art of becoming a "son of God" is a long, hard task.*
Many miss the mark of such a calling. Man is sinful and needs
conversion. I am at times terribly disturbed about human nature as to why it has a stubborn note of egocentricity which

---

[*] *Process and Reality* (New York: The Macmillan Co., 1929), p. 327.

I BELIEVE IN MAN

causes its sinfulness. Nevertheless I am confident that within most individuals this sinfulness can be eradicated if their potentialities can be harnessed to the proper motivations. Perhaps at the end of the nineteenth century some could sing with Swinburne, "Glory to Man in the highest, for Man is the Master of Things!" But the holocaust of two world wars within one generation, caustically tempered by the superficial, depressing twenty-five years between the two wars, has caused many today to have a deflated confidence in man.

European theology during the last thirty years has in particular had a pessimism toward human nature. This attitude toward man's sinfulness has resulted largely from the crisis school of theologians, led mainly by Karl Barth. Barth himself was largely influenced by Calvin and Kierkegaard. Certainly today a person of intellectual sanity cannot swear allegiance to Swinburne's easy optimism regarding man. On the other hand, the pessimism of crisis theology seems untrue to the main currents of the Christian ideology. Walter Horton has acutely expressed an attitude which seems close to the Christian position:

Some Christian thinkers have seen in this current deflation or devaluation of man the means of inducing in our contemporaries a mood of humility meet for repentance. To deepen man's self-distrust seems like the quickest and most efficacious way of leading them to trust in God—or at least the most opportune way at the moment—and so there are found many Christian pessimists in our time, ever ready to answer the wails of secular pessimists with antiphonal groans, when the plight of modern man comes up for discussion. Yet it is a dangerous stratagem to exalt God at the expense of man; almost, though not quite so dangerous as to exalt man at the expense of God. Faith in God and faith in man are so interdependent that we cannot utterly despair of man without undermining faith in God, just as we cannot ignore God without undermining faith in man. If the godless secularism of modern times leads inevitably to that loss of trust in humanity which is so evident today, the attempt to bludgeon man into abject submission to God may lead with equal logicality to a new wave of atheism. . . .

17

CREDO—FUNDAMENTAL CHRISTIAN BELIEFS

The Christian gospel, when rightly received, humbles man to a sense of grateful dependence upon the power, grace, and forgiveness of God; it does not humiliate him nor break his spirit. . . . But in the same breath, it declares that man is God's child, made in the divine image, destined for an exalted post, as God's vicegerent on this planet, so soon as he learns to find his joy in obedience to his Father's will.[7]

God's *agape* (redemptive love) working in the life of man is the way to God's high purpose for each Christian. It is symbolized in the life of a saint!

6. *As modern man looks at himself through Christian theistic eyes, he believes that possible sainthood lies in every person,* even though the struggle to become a Christian saint is long and arduous. His belief in man's possible attainment of sainthood is based on two premises; (1) he has faith in man's potentialities for greatness even though the image of God in him is distorted; (2) he believes in a God of tremendous energy and mercy (*agape*) who dynamically seeks to help man achieve the goal of the saint. The Christian theist is neither pessimistic nor optimistic about man; he is melioristic, believing that there is a Christlikeness in all of us which by a combination of human and divine effort can be fanned into the life of a saint. With Leon Bloy he feels that "there is only one sorrow, not to be a saint."

Some traits of the Christian saint as the ideal man are these: (1) His life is saturated with an intense love for the Christian religion as a way of adjusting himself to himself, to his fellow men, to nature, and to God. He is a "religion-intoxicated" person! (2) He lives with a joyous, radiant, carefree freedom because his life is totally dependent upon God. "A saint is a person who has quit worrying about himself," because his life is centered in God. (3) He emulates Christ in everything he does. Each day he offers a prayer at dawn, "May the image of Christ radiate through me this day in every life situation."

[7] *The Christian Understanding of Man* (Oxford Conference report; Chicago: Willett, Clark & Co., 1938), pp. 219-20.

18

(4) He freely opens his life to God's *agape* (redemptive, free-giving love), and as the recipient of God's *agape* he volunteers to help the needy, the lost, the unfortunate, the unhappy. He volunteers to help bear the burdens of his fellow men and thus fulfills the spiritual laws of God. (5) He looks upon Christianity as not merely a theoretical ideal; for him it is a practical way of living with individuals in an un-Christian society. It is more than an interim ethic. Like St. Francis he does "not love humanity, but men." (6) He believes that the Kingdom of God can come into history. But it must continue in him as it began in Christ. With Jacques Maritain he concurs that he must "purify the springs of history within his own heart." (7) He has a continuous humility. Like Katharine Mansfield looking at her writings shortly before her death and saying beautifully, "Not one of these dare I show to God," he feels that his best is always minute as compared with God's majestic and holy perfection. (8) He looks wistfully into the eyes of every person, regardless of race, color, creed, or nation, as a brother in whom the potentialities of a Christian saint lie.

Yes, I believe in man—and especially the Christian man as the type of person who must labor for the postwar world to become more like God's Kingdom. "Saints are men the light shines through"—especially the light of one who was the Light of the world. The degree to which that light will radiate through Christian men and women will determine their effectiveness as they play their roles as emissaries of God's Kingdom.

In the profound utterance of the *Talmud*, I believe that as long as there are thirty righteous men in any generation there is hope for tomorrow's world—because as I believe in man I am led to believe also in God, who labors with men for the Kingdom!

I BELIEVE IN GOD

PITIRIM SOROKIN, PROFESSOR OF SOCIOLOGY AT HARVARD UNI-
versity, paints two types of people in the history of civilization. One type of people, as it has met famine, war, and pestilence, has reacted to such catastrophes with cynicism, despair, and bestial living. The other type has arisen to heights
of great moral behavior and deep devotion to ideals. Sorokin
concludes that the diverse reactions to similar situations have
been caused by the structure of values for which the different
groups have lived. The Jewish-Christian tradition exemplifies
a people who have met their trials with triumphant courage
and high idealism, *because they believe in God!* [1]
What a person believes about God has a deep, abiding
effect on what a person feels about life. Tolstoy has shown how
thoughts about God control the creative urge for man's constructive living. After years of despair in which he cherished
suicide, he began to find whenever he *thought* about God
that a new release of energy crept into him. After such experiences of God he concluded, "There arose in me, with this
thought, glad aspirations towards life. Everything in me awoke
and received a meaning. . . . Why do I look farther? a voice
within me asked. He is there: he, without whom one cannot live. To acknowledge God and to live are one and the
same thing. God is what life is. Well, then! live, seek God,
and there will be no life without him." [2]

[1] *Man and Society in Calamity* (New York: E. P. Dutton & Co., 1942).
[2] Quoted by William James, *The Varieties of Religious Experience* (New
York: Longmans, Green & Co., 1915), p. 185.

20

I BELIEVE IN GOD

What a person believes about God is a major enterprise in each man's life. What, then, does a modern Christian believe about God?

1. *"In the beginning God"—this is the starting place* for any Christian *credo*. God is not the imaginative creation of men as something to satisfy their wishful thinking; rather man and the universe are caused by God, and are dependent on him for their continued existence. God is the Life of the Universe, controlling the stars in their courses; yet he is as close to men as the breath they breathe. He is out where the morning stars sing together, yet he is actively immanent in the life about us. "He is involved in the hazard of his creation. He is striving mightily to produce a perfect display in the world of sense-perception, of his own true nature." [3]

When we speak of God as the "Life of the Universe" we are thinking of the universe in an organic sense. Just as every individual has a spirit of life which knits the cells of his body into an organic unity, God is the Life of the Universe which "holds the universe together" and keeps all parts of the universe interrelated. Everything in the universe depends upon God for its sustenance, and the manner in which man and nature adjust themselves to the sustaining life of God causes the human or natural health of each part of the universe.

I know of no place where the initial Christian definition of God is more succinctly portrayed than in these words of Henry S. Coffin:

God is to me that creative Force, behind and in the universe, who manifests himself as energy, as life, as order, as beauty, as thought, as conscience, as love, and who is self-revealed supremely in the creative Person of Jesus of Nazareth, and operative in all Jesus-like movements in the world today.

In the physical universe I see Him as energy—the energy of whirling electrons which compose light, and which build up the

[3] K. F. Mather, *Science in Search of God* (New York: Henry Holt & Co., 1928), pp. 69-70.

21

planets, of which our earth is one. I see Him in upsurging life, which assumes innumerable forms in plants and creatures, forms that change in adaptation to changing conditions. And in this vast and unceasing outflow of energy and life I see Him in universally present order and beauty. . . . The "laws of nature" which we discover and formulate are our descriptions of the ways in which we find that God consistently works. . . . Poets, artists, and musicians, who are "priests of the wonder and bloom of the world," are to me interpreters of God, who is Beauty, as well as Energy, Life, and Order.[4]

In September, 1715, at the funeral services of Louis XIV of France in the Cathedral of Notre Dame, the people of France awaited the bishop's eulogy of their king. When the moment arrived for the eulogy, the bishop said four words, "Only—God—is—great!" That statement is the starting place for the Christian's view of God!

2. *The contemporary Christian understands the character of God most deeply through the insights of Jesus.* Jesus never attempted to prove God's existence for his listeners; he assumed' that they naturally believed in the God of "Abraham, Isaac, and Jacob," and accepted the attributes of God defined by the great prophets of Israel. Recently a student in an American college said that he wished chapel speakers would cease trying to *prove* God's existence for the students, and instead show them how they might *find* God. Jesus would have pleased that student, because Jesus spent most of his time telling his followers about the God they believed in and how he might be experientially real in their lives. He said to them, "The kingdom of God is within you."

Jesus' understanding of God paralleled the views of Hosea, Isaiah, Jeremiah, and Second Isaiah. These men showed to him a God of mercy, forgiveness, majestic energy, and holiness, who meets each individual "within his heart," and who is the God of all humanity. Likewise a Christian today thinks

---

[4] Joseph Fort Newton, ed., *My Idea of God* (Boston: Little, Brown & Co., 1926), pp. 125-26.

I BELIEVE IN GOD

of God as the Life of the Universe, related to all creatures, and possessing *mercy* and *holiness*.

The *mercy* or *love* of God, as seen through Jesus' eyes, is *agape*. This signifies a kind of love which God pours out upon the undeserving, the unlovely, the unattractive in order that he can remedy the weakness and emptiness of men; it "is a free gift, a salvation which is the work of divine love . . . is unselfish love, which 'seeketh not its own,' and freely spends itself . . . is God's way to man . . . is self-giving . . . comes down from above."[5] It is the kind of love which God possesses as he *seeks out* the lost, the sinful, the hopeless. It means that at "the heart of the universe" there is a Great Companion who is trying to find us even more than we are trying to find him! Out of his deep mercy he infinitely forgives the repentant.

Holiness usually signifies a quality of goodness carried to its highest degree. Many people qualify God as being absolutely good when they reverence him as holy. The word does mean perfect goodness, but it also means something deeper and higher! It attaches to God's goodness the traits of tremendous mystery, majesty, magnificence, infinite energy. God is the eternal God of the infinite universe whom man holds in awe. By contrast, man in his humility feels his littleness as a creature living on this tiny planet for a few decades.

A few years ago I read *Dreams of an Astronomer* by Camille Flammarion, in which he tells of going to Mars (37,-000,000 miles away), and then to Neptune (2,500,000,000 miles away), then to the nearest light-star, Alpha Centauri (25,000,000,000 miles away), and then out into infinite space, on—and on—and on—where he finally learned that our little second-rate planet, related to a second-rate sun, is but a tiny room in a solar mansion. Then as I thought of God's Spirit as related to every area of this infinite universe, the littleness of

[5] Anders Nygren, *Agape and Eros* (New York: The Macmillan Co., 1932), p. 165.

my creature nature overwhelmed me; I felt my humility—
I understood what the holiness of God really means!

3. *The Christian idea of God is defined, but not confined,
in Jesus.* A Hindu converted to Christianity said, "God is too
great an idea for me to grasp. But when I think about Jesus,
he seems to hold my universe steady." God is too great a concept for most of us to fathom; we need something tangible
and known from which we can attempt to understand the
intangible and the unknown. As the early Christians looked
at the tangible and the known in the life and spirit of Jesus,
they said, "We believe that we who have seen the Spirit in
the Son have seen the Spirit in the Father." This was the
basis for the concept of the Incarnation.

When we say that God's Spirit was incarnate in Jesus Christ,
we do not mean to say that *all* of God's Spirit was incarnate
in him—only that immanent part of God's Spirit which relates itself to the religious-social-moral relations of men with
God and men with men. What God is like as one who rules
out where galaxies exist, Jesus did not say; what God is like
as the creator of mathematical axioms and radioactive rays,
Jesus did not teach. God as a "being of primordial nature" [6]
or a Great Mathematician[7] were not concerns of Jesus. Jesus
mainly taught regarding the way God's reign could come
spiritually and morally into the hearts of men living here on
this planet; he believed that God's reign was here in their
midst, whether they recognized it or not, and that God's reign
would come fully into history at some future time. His own
life showed what all lives would be like when God's reign
had arrived. He had allowed such a reign to become incarnate
in him.

4. *The Christian believes that his life is never detached from
the life of God in the universe.* The life of God is always
touching the life of man, at least below the plane of consciousness. (Shall we call it "the realm of the subconscious"?) There

[6] Whitehead, *Process and Reality,* pp. 75-76.
[7] Sir James Hopwood Jeans, *The Mysterious Universe* (New York: The
Macmillan Co., 1937), p. 165.

are various ways by which man becomes aware of the personal immanence of the Overspirit which hovers in and around the life of man. Music, poetry, dutiful acts, prayer, rational reflection, merciful attitudes toward humanity are all means by which man becomes more spiritually aware that his spirit has a close attachment to God's Spirit. However, if man wishes to scale the heights in his feeling of close communion with the Spirit of God, he can discipline his intuition (feeling) to appreciate these high experiences. The more his feelings are schooled to emerge from the lower planes of appreciating God, the more he feels his sense of mystical unity with the Infinite Spirit from whom man is never detached. All of these experiences are ways of realizing what Brother Lawrence called "practicing the presence of God."

5. *The Christian believes that God's goodness and wisdom are never limited,* even though the power of God is momentarily limited by real freedom which God has given to men. Some Christians are agreed that God is further momentarily limited by natural evils, such as hurricanes and volcanoes, since God abides by the laws of the universe, and will not set aside or change the laws of nature so that these evils be avoided. To God, all limitations of his power are spurs for divine-human activity for working out his eternal plan on this planet. They stimulate men both to seek divine companionship and to bear the burdens of one another, and thus to fulfill the spiritual laws of the universe. The Christian believes that God as the Great Companion suffers with men—"the Cross [is] in the eternal nature of God" [8]—but out of this companionship of divine-human problem bearing come the highest, most rugged, and most purposive types of persons. It is the way Christlike characters are made. It is the manner by which God and man, working eternally together on this planet, will eventually make it a community of redemptive love.

[8] E. S. Brightman, *The Problem of God* (New York: Abingdon Press, 1930), p. 189.

6. *Is God a Trinity?* Recently my son and I visited a neighbor who is an amateur astronomer—yet very expert. He showed us the moon, various stars, and finally a galaxy which lies beyond our own. That galaxy is presumed to be 30,000 light-years from our galaxy. Such a figure in terms of miles was for me but an emotional symbol of *distance;* I could not attempt to rationalize what it meant!

Twenty years ago I heard Fritz Kreisler play his violin in the Auditorium Theater in Chicago on a Sunday afternoon. Although I sat high in the balconies, as I heard him play to a vast audience and the strains from his violin came to me, they struck something within me that afternoon; and I walked out onto Michigan Boulevard with a more adventurous, wistful look in my eyes. Something happened to me in that experience of *beauty* which I could not rationalize.

What I have mentioned regarding my experiences of distance and beauty as emotional symbols yet not rationalized conclusions is true of trinitarian theologians as they have tried to concern themselves with Jesus' clarification of God's meaning to humanity. The Trinity is an emotional symbol of Christian faith rather than a clearly defined intellectual concept. No great theologian has ever discerned the Trinity otherwise.

The basis for trinitarian thought goes to the Gospel of John, written about A.D. 100 at Ephesus. It was an attempt to translate the religion *of* Jesus into the religion *about* Jesus, so that Jesus could be understood by a Hellenistic audience in terms of Christian mysticism. John's argument runs as follows: God and Christ (the Divine Word) existed before the world was made. When God made the world, Christ was the co-creator. God's Spirit was always in the world for men to know, but it was too tremendous a concept for the mind of finite man to understand. Men needed something tangible in order to understand the infinite mystery of God. So the Spirit of Christ (the Word) became flesh in the physical person of Jesus, dwelling among men for a short time in Palestine. For those who learned to know God through him, life

26

became a new experience of joy, strength, purpose, spiritual adventure. Through Jesus, God's Spirit had come consciously close to them. Even after Jesus' death they realized that the intimate closeness of God's Spirit still hovered about them as the merciful, life-giving energy of the universe. Without Jesus' having taught about and clarified the close intimacy (immanence) of God's Spirit, God would have remained far away (transcendent). It was Jesus as his particular "Son" who had made them realize the continuing nearness of God's Spirit (termed the "Holy Spirit").

Today as Christian theists we think of God as the Life of the Universe, who is always near us. Let us say that this Life ever touches us at the level of the subconscious—this personal immanence of his Spirit in symbolic language is the *Holy Spirit*. This Life is everywhere in the universe, out among the farthest galaxies, but for us it is warmly near as the personal Life which is about us and within us. It strengthens, supports, sustains, and guides us as a *Father*—Jesus uses the symbol of "Father" 153 times in the gospel reports. Our clarity and understanding of God as a near, fatherly, personal Spirit of *agape* has come to us as a spiritual heritage because Jesus not only taught what God was like, but also lived—as his first followers believed—what God was like. He lived as a *Son*, showing us through the Christian centuries how we too may share the same sonship! Is not the depth of our Christian *credo* based on this belief?

Many Christians today are intellectually unitarians, believing that God is one and that Jesus as a Galilean carpenter and prophet so obeyed the will of God that God's will and spirit shone serenely through him. What deeper values people may see in the formula of the Trinity to enrich their religious experiences must remain a gesture of their desire for emotional symbolism. "Life is [often] deeper than logic." Some people deeply cherish the rich symbolism of the language of the Trinity, while others discern words as "Father" and "Son" as dignified, richly endowed terms to describe the immanence of God in a theistic framework. In either instance we intuit

27

the deep religious meaning of the Christian faith, reverencing the figure of Jesus as the one who left profound and pragmatic insights into the Spirit of God which we too appreciate as his twentieth-century disciples.

While Benjamin Franklin was seeking French support for the Revolution, the aged Voltaire returned to Paris after an absence of many years. The American representative called to pay his respects to the man all France was acclaiming, taking with him his grandson, who was serving as his secretary. The most memorable words uttered in that meeting of the two famed philosophers were the blessing Voltaire gave to young Franklin. Placing his hands on the youth's head he spoke: "My child, God and liberty! Recollect those two words."

Today as the Christian lives in a world of competing ideologies, may he not forget these words of Voltaire. They are basically involved in the Christian's hope for this world's becoming God's Kingdom. They are at the heart of Christian sainthood, about which Emily Herman writes:

[The saints] always seemed to hit the mark; every bit of their life *told;* their simplest actions had a distinction, an exquisiteness which suggested the artist. The reason is not far to seek. Their sainthood lay in their habit of referring the smallest actions to God. They lived in God; they acted from a pure motive of love towards God. They were as free from self-regard as from slavery to the good opinion of others. God saw and God rewarded: what else needed they? . . . Hence the inalienable dignity of these meek, quiet figures that seem to produce such marvellous effects with such humble materials.[9]

Can a Christian do less than *believe* in God—and then *act* his role as God's instrument of *agape* in a needy world? Surely the hour of decision has arrived when each of us must answer and act!

Creative Prayer (New York: George H. Doran, 1925), p. 31. By permission of Harper & Bros.

I BELIEVE IN JESUS CHRIST

Anatole France's short story "the procurator of judaea" portrays Pilate in his old age meeting in Italy a friend, Aelius Lamia, with whom he had shared many experiences in Palestine. After a long conversation about Palestinian events which Pilate declares "are as vividly present to me as if they had happened yesterday," Lamia mentions having heard of an unusual character named Jesus and asks, "Pontius, do you remember anything about the man?"

Pilate hesitatingly answers, "Jesus? . . . Jesus—of Nazareth? I cannot call him to mind."

It is one of life's necessities that Christians do take time to "call Jesus to mind." As modern men look into their mysterious universe, as did the wise men of old, and discern the nearest light-star, Alpha Centauri, twenty-five billion miles away, their need of a "savior" is just as basic as that of the first-century wise men guided by the star in the east. Perhaps their need is even deeper!

Jesus' grandeur perennially affects artist, musician, and theologian, who in turn inspire us as they depict him. It is a momentous experience to sit in the small room in a Dresden gallery where Raphael's "Sistine Madonna" hangs in quiet beauty. One's soul is lifted into eternity as one listens to Handel's *Messiah*. To observe the thousands of books in a theological library written about Jesus fills one with a feeling of wonder.

As much as I am moved by the mystery of human existence, I find myself even more awed when I ponder the person of

29

CREDO—FUNDAMENTAL CHRISTIAN BELIEFS

Jesus Christ. Dean Case expresses the problem clearly when he says that Jesus has been the enigma of the centuries to both saint and skeptic. He is the most irrationally intriguing object of human quest yet to walk in mystery on this little planet. If we today find his way of life and his conception of God so satisfying, is it any wonder that his followers of the first century adorned his name with titles such as "Christ," "Son of God," "Lord," "Logos," and "Saviour"?

What can we believe about Jesus?

1. *Jesus was a historical person who lived on Palestinian soil, who was crucified under Pontius Pilate in Judea about* A.D. 30. Jesus is not an adaptation of the Babylonian Gilgamesh epic on Jewish soil; he is not merely the personification of a social movement which was Roman in origin and Jewish in form; he is not the mythical hero of a sacred Jewish drama in which the father sacrifices a god for the salvation of humanity; he is not a synthetic figure in a drama drawn from the Oriental mystery religions.[1] No established New Testament scholar today views Jesus other than as a real, historical person. Even a radical New Testament critic like Rudolf Bultmann concludes, "Jesus actually lived as a rabbi."[2] Bultmann's statement may not satisfy one's Christological interpretation of Jesus; it does, however, assert Jesus' historical reality.

2. *While we do not have any "photographs" of the historical Jesus in the New Testament writings, we do have significant "portraits" of him artistically painted.* The Epistle to the Hebrews depicts Jesus as the ideal high priest and sacrifice of a worship system. The book of Revelation paints him as one who will return to lead the righteous forces against Antichrist and the evil forces at Armageddon. Paul, in giving us his views of the crucified and risen Christ, mentions only a few facts about the historical Jesus—he was born of woman, of the line of David, had brothers and sisters, was crucified, dead,

[1] The theories respectively of Jensen, Kalthoff, Robertson, and Drews. See C. Guignebert, *Jesus* (New York: Alfred A. Knopf, 1935), pp. 63-75.

[2] *Jesus and the Word* (New York: Charles Scribner's Sons, 1934). p. 58.

buried, and resurrected. Paul emphasizes Jesus as a real historical person who became the Christ of experience. The Gospel of John gives a more accurate portrait of the historical Jesus than is found in Paul's writings, yet less accurate than is observed in the Synoptic Gospels—Matthew, Mark, and Luke. The Gospel of John uses some historical stories about Jesus, not to preserve accurate historical data, but to show how believers should become integral members of the mystical Christian community.

Matthew, Mark, and Luke give us the clearest pictures of the historical Jesus, yet in each of these Gospels facts and beliefs are intricately woven together. These facts and beliefs are so closely fabricated that the bare Jesus of history cannot with the scholars' tools be completely detached from the Christ of faith. What a Christian of the first century *believed* about Jesus was almost as important as what he *knew* about Jesus. Such a combination of facts and beliefs is to be expected, since no New Testament interpretation of Jesus was written by a nonbeliever. Dibelius remarks that each Gospel was composed by an individual who possessed the "eye of faith." The interpreters never wrote their Gospels about *Jesus;* they were about Jesus *Christ.*

The "portraits" of Jesus in the twenty-seven New Testament writings do not show Jesus as a stereotyped person, easily interpreted by one theological pattern. The New Testament contains at least *seven* distinct theologies about Jesus, each a profound attempt to explain the mystery of Jesus. Jesus was too big and too complex to be captured by one theological mold. The uniqueness of his personality intrigued first-century theologians of every background to explain him, and the same diversity of interpretation has persisted through the centuries.

3. *Jesus was a Jew, born into the family of a carpenter; he had brothers and sisters; he was reared in the Law and the Prophets, the sacred scriptures of the Jews.* About 95 per cent of Jesus' ethical teachings are found in the Torah (Law) and the rabbinical teachings, but he was able to cull the important ethical teachings from a vast storehouse of aged moral

31

and ceremonial ideas. Like every Jew, Jesus loved the Torah; it was a lamp unto his feet and a light unto his path. He found the two greatest commandments, "Love thy God" (Deut. 6:5) and "Love thy neighbor" (Lev. 19:18), in the Torah. His idea of God as a holy, merciful, judging, immanent Father, who would give his Kingdom to faithful, repentant people, was found amid prophets like Amos, Hosea, Isaiah, Jeremiah, and Second Isaiah.

Yet there was something about the person of Jesus which gave a new impression to the ideas which he quoted from the Law and the Prophets. Ethical teachings uttered for centuries by scribes and teachers seemed more distinctly the will of God because Jesus spoke them; the Sermon on the Mount (Matt. 5–7) as an ethical code became God's ultimate demand for men to follow when Jesus reiterated its precepts, "for he taught them as one having authority, and not as the scribes." As he spoke about God, he seemed to be one who not only told about the immanent Spirit of God in the life of men— he seemed to live that kind of Spirit within himself. Because his life and his religious teachings seemed in accord, his followers said of him, "He is the Christ"—that is, God's Spirit has inwardly "anointed" the spirit of Jesus—"We believe that we who have seen the spirit in the Son have seen the Spirit of the Father." Consequently, with Jesus began the long-expected reign of God in the life of man, and from his life and teachings his followers then and now have found how they too may inherit the Kingdom of God within their lives.

Jesus was a Jew who belonged organically to Judaism; he owed his religious inheritance and stimulus to the religious teachers and prophets of Judaism. What he said and did, however, could not be held within the confines of any racial group, for he keenly interpreted those religious-ethical values which are always essential to all men. C. H. Dodd significantly states this idea:

We take therefore the work and influence of Jesus Christ in their

I BELIEVE IN JESUS CHRIST

full scope as the climax of that whole complex process which we have traced in the Bible, and we conclude that the process itself is so intimately and dynamically related to all that we cannot but hold to be of the highest spiritual worth, that we must recognize it in the fullest sense as a revelation of God, a revelation whose unique quality is measured by the uniqueness of Jesus Christ Himself and His relation to the human race.[8]

4. *Because of the profound effect Jesus left upon his followers, especially after the resurrection experiences, the New Testament writings contain several significant Christological interpretations regarding him.* (1) Some believed that God had adopted Jesus as the Son of God at his baptism. The Gospel of Mark—written about A.D. 70—begins with the baptism, at which "he saw the heavens opened, and the Spirit, like a dove, descending upon him: and there came a voice from heaven, saying, Thou art my beloved Son, in whom I am well pleased." Theologians call this the "Adoptionist" theory. (2) Perhaps as a reaction to Jesus' adoption by God at the baptism, the Gospels of Matthew and Luke—written about A.D. 85—look upon Jesus as one *born* into the world as a savior. These two Gospels attempt to explain Jesus' sinless nature through his being born of a virgin mother who conceived the Holy Spirit, thus ruling out a human father. The question arose in the minds of first-century theologians, "How could Jesus be perfect; for are not all people related to Adam, and did not Adam's pride allow sin to enter the human race? And if Jesus had been biologically related to Adam, would not he have been sinful as other men?" But the doctrine of the Virgin Birth, they believed, eliminated the taint of original sin from Jesus. Later, in the thirteenth century, after scholars had discussed the possibility of sin's being inherited through the mother, the doctrine of the Immaculate Conception was adopted. This stated that at Mary's birth a miracle happened so that original sin was removed from her. (3) The Gospel of John—written about A.D. 100—

[8] *The Authority of the Bible* (New York: Harper & Bros., 1929), p. 285.

33

goes more deeply into the theological explanation of the mystery of Jesus. It resorts to the "Logos" interpretation, which says that before God created the world, God and the Logos coexisted; that when God created the world, the Logos was the cocreator; that in the person of Jesus Christ the Logos—or the Spirit of God—became flesh, giving spiritual light to those who had been dwelling in spiritual darkness. After being among men in Palestine for a few years the Logos returned to the bosom of the Father; yet his Spirit remained among men as the Comforter—the Spirit of Truth. For those believers who found this Comforter, eternal life seemed a present qualitative possession.

These views of Jesus Christ still hold significance for many contemporary thinkers. Whether Jesus possessed a unique relationship with God before the world was made—as the divine Logos—or became a savior at the time of his birth, or achieved a unique relationship with God at his baptism cannot be scientifically proved. The view a person holds must be a gesture of faith based on what he deems the soundest factual foundation. And faith must always have close connection to facts that seem rationally coherent and experientially pragmatic.

Some today prefer to think of Jesus mainly as a great *prophet*. F. C. Grant holds to such a view:

Was Jesus then only a prophet? It may be a hard saying, but after all "prophet" is only one more historical category—and Jesus was unique. In fact, on Jewish lips "prophet" was the highest possible category, next to God himself. . . . Jesus the prophet, the Teacher sent from God, seems to me not only to fit far better the actual historical situation reflected in the Gospels, but also to provide a far more probable mode of the Incarnation than any category drawn from apocalyptic Messianism.[4]

For my own Christological appreciation of Jesus I have framed my ideas thus: Ordinary categories lack adequacy in

[4] "Form Criticism and the Christian Faith," *Journal of Bible and Religion*, February, 1939.

describing Jesus. That he belongs organically to history none would deny; both his prophetic continuity with Jewish tradition and his integral relationship to the last nineteen hundred years establish this note. Yet Jesus transcends history both in his relation to God and in the way he has inspired man; to rule out this qualitative transcendence is to lack historical perspective. Jesus and we are both organically members of the same universe. It is his *degree* of relationship to God which causes his difference from us. The more we develop through his ways a mystical relationship to God, the more we understand the mystery of his being as a "savior." Whatever titles we may use to adorn his name are but symbolic nomenclatures born out of the ways his spirit affects our spirits.[5]

5. *Jesus' greatness lies in the way he has brought to man a perennial gospel of salvation by which man has been able to adjust himself to himself, to his fellow men, and to God.* Emerson once said that "the lesson of life is to learn what the centuries have to say to the hours." Jesus was a first-century Jew, but his message has resounded as real and virile "over the changing centuries because he spoke to unchanging needs of the heart of man." [6] His message has remained fresh for every age when men have taken time to understand and live its basic meanings.

In Eugene O'Neill's *Days Without End,* John Loving, a Roman Catholic boy, loses his faith. One day in conversation with Father Beaird, John Loving remarks, "A new savior must be born who will reveal to us how we can be saved from ourselves, so that we can be free of the past and inherit the future and not perish by it." To which Father Beaird replies, "You are forgetting that men have such a savior, Jack. All they need is to remember him." That Father Beaird

[5] See Kepler, "Modernism Seeks Depth," *Journal of Bible and Religion,* February, 1939.

[6] C. T. Craig, *Jesus in Our Teaching* (New York: Abingdon Press, 1931), p. 116.

was correct in his reference to Jesus several contemporary New Testament scholars concur.

C. H. Dodd:

When moral and religious advance is made, it is not true to say that it antiquates the teaching of Jesus; on the contrary, it presents itself as a fresh unfolding of what Jesus meant. The more His Gospel goes out into the wider world, the more clearly does it exhibit its universal character. . . . For our present purpose it is enough to record that after many centuries of historical vicissitudes His word is still current, and fertile of new truth.[7]

Martin Dibelius:

The Sermon on the Mount does not speak of human or worldly conditions but only of God's eternal will. . . . We are not able *to perform* it in its full scope, but we are able to be transformed by it.[8]

Albert Schweitzer:

He comes to us as One unknown, without a name, as of old, by the lake-side, He came to those men who knew Him not. He speaks to us the same word: "Follow thou me!" and sets us to the tasks which He has to fulfil for our time. He commands. And to those who obey Him, whether they be wise or simple, He will reveal Himself in the toils, the conflicts, the sufferings which they shall pass through in His fellowship, and, as an ineffable mystery, they shall learn in their own experience Who He is.[9]

The grandeur of Jesus cannot be externally proved by a dogma, a Christological title, a book, or a council; his greatness is measured by the way his insights into spiritual values

[7] *The Authority of the Bible*, pp. 282, 283.
[8] *The Sermon on the Mount* (New York: Charles Scribner's Sons, 1940), p. 136.
[9] *The Quest of the Historical Jesus* (New York: The Macmillan Co., 1910), p. 401.

36

continue to affect the lives of men. We continue to call him Lord—and I humbly yet proudly number myself among such believers—because in the Christian faith he is still "the way, and the truth, and the life." With Vachel Lindsay many of us in this dark hour of civilization are able to affirm as the cornerstone of our *credo:*

> This is our faith tremendous,—
> Our wild hope, who shall scorn,—
> That in the name of Jesus
> The world shall be reborn! [10]

[10] "Foreign Missions in Battle Array," from *Collected Poems* (New York: The Macmillan Co., 1925).

I BELIEVE IN THE RELIGION OF JESUS

SEVERAL YEARS AGO DR. JAMES R. ANGELL, THEN PRESIDENT OF Yale University, gave the baccalaureate address at Columbia University. While walking with the Columbia University faculty into the chapel where the exercises were to be held, he noticed on the outside of the chapel door the word "PUSH." He saw a sermon in that word, and decided to weave it into his morning talk as the key of his advice to the Columbia graduates. In introducing his address he said, "I am taking my text this morning, not from a philosopher, a literateur, or a biblical writer. Rather I have taken it from the one word engraved on the door of this great chapel, and offer it to you as the one thing each of you needs most when you leave the corridors of this university for the amphitheater of the world." Whereupon several of the seniors, sitting near the back of the chapel, turned around and saw inscribed—on the *inside* of the chapel door—"PULL."

As we turn this homily from the facile to the serious, man's life, if it be complete, *is* highly sensitized by his response to both the push and the pull of life: the *push* is the inner drive or motivation man has for being religious, while the *pull* is that outside of man which encourages or supports man in his good endeavors. Professor Harris F. Rall in his book *Christianity* speaks of these two essentials in religion:

We may call the needs of man the "push" of religion, that which impels man from behind. But there is a "pull" of religion also. Religion is not merely desire, it is response. As the physical

38

universe by its stimulus has created our organs of sense perception, and has called forth such varied responses in man as the scientific knowledge of its order and the creative control of its forces, so the impact of this spiritual world has brought forth religion. It has itself created the needs for which it affords satisfaction. . . . Religion involves the belief in a higher world which has the answer to our needs.[1]

Men have perennially attempted to define religion, and their definitions have been as diverse as those of Alfred N. Whitehead and A. Eustace Haydon. Says Professor Whitehead, "Religion is what one does with one's solitariness"[2]—an *individual* stress. Dr. Haydon looks upon religion as "a shared quest of the good life"[3]—the *social* stress. Dr. Harry Emerson Fosdick defines religion more comprehensively in these words: "Religion at its source is personal adventure on a way of living."[4] While such a definition is a bit general, it nevertheless sees religion in its totality as something tremendous in the life of man. A good definition must be all-inclusive, touching four wide areas of man's experience: (1) man's relationship to himself (the *psychological* aspect); (2) man's relationship to his fellow men (the *ethical* aspect); (3) man's relationship to God (the *theological* aspect); (4) man's relationship to the problems of life which are not brought directly upon him by himself, his fellow men, or God; we call them the problems caused by the natural world (an area including the *psychological,* the *ethical,* and the *theological* aspects as man attempts to meet these problems).

It is interesting to note that when Professor Charles S. Braden sent a questionnaire to people of all ages and theological backgrounds with sixty-five possible reasons as to why they were religious, the six leading answers related themselves to the four main areas just mentioned: (1) religion

[1] *Christianity* (New York: Charles Scribner's Sons, 1940), pp. 5, 6.
[2] *Religion in the Making* (New York: The Macmillan Co., 1926), p. 16.
[3] *The Quest of the Ages* (New York: Harper & Bros., 1929), p. ix.
[4] *Adventurous Living* (New York: Harper & Bros., 1926), p. 1.

39

brings meaning to life; (2) religion brings help in time of stress; (3) religion motivates human kindness; (4) religion stimulates a person to better things; (5) religion furnishes a person with a moral ideal; (6) religion excites thoughtful people to believe in God and to worship him.

It is my privilege to make a survey of the world's living religions two or three times a year. I always try to approach every world religion—whether Hinduism, Buddhism, Taoism, Christianity, Confucianism, Judaism, Zoroastrianism, or Islam —with an open mind and with complete tolerance; and I must confess that I find relative good in every religion. After I make each survey I am always impressed with two facts: (1) Christianity offers the best *balance* of any of the religions, in so far as the four norms for a good religion are concerned; (2) since Jesus not only *taught* his intriguing ideas about religion, but *lived* them as well, he leaves a magnetic charm for others to try his insights—they were shown by him as possible in the kind of a universe in which we live.

Dr. Harry E. Barnes in *The Twilight of Christianity*, written nearly twenty years ago, developed the thesis that Jesus was outmoded, that his religion belonged to a first-century Oriental civilization in a nomadic handicraft culture, that Jesus never wandered more than a few miles from his home town and had only a provincial scope. Dr. Barnes felt that we ought to pay less attention to Jesus than to twentieth-century American thinkers, with their feel of an Occidental machine age and their comprehension of an international pattern of events. Among the men of the present day with this touch of modernity Barnes mentioned Kirby Page, Reinhold Niebuhr, Sherwood Eddy, and Bishop Francis McConnell; but little did Barnes realize that all of these men are the results of a tradition—in their homes, their environments, their colleges, their churches, their seminaries—all begun and stimulated by Jesus. Their total adjustments and the culture they inherit as twentieth-century Americans are largely due to the insights of Jesus in regard to man, society, God, and the problems caused by nature. As these men have added their contributions to

40

I BELIEVE IN THE RELIGION OF JESUS

Jesus' ethical-religious stimulus, they have led us into what Clarence T. Craig calls Christian conduct: "Conduct is Christian when in response to God's forgiving grace men seek to solve their human problems according to the principle of love, using the guidance of Jesus, the best ethical experience of the race, and the fullest possible contemporary knowledge of facts." [5]

How does Jesus' religion help man in his total Christian conduct?

1. *Jesus' religion adjusts man to himself*—the psychological aspect. While fear, a sense of guilt, and the bearing of resentments are the chief "evils which lay waste life," they are really the by-products of self-centeredness; and selfishness is the central evil contributing to man's inability to get along with himself. Dr. William Burnham has said that until a child is eight years of age, his business as a child is to be selfish, but after that period he must get away from self-centeredness, else he will never be a maturely integrated personality. Today our hospitals and asylums are filled with people who have carelessly become inflated egoists. The superintendent of an asylum in Ibsen's *Peer Gynt* vividly describes this selfish evil in the inmates:

> Beside themselves? Oh no, you're wrong.
> It's here that men are most themselves—
> Themselves and nothing but themselves—
> Sailing with outspread sails of self.
> Each shuts himself in a cask of self,
> The cask stopped with a bung of self,
> And seasoned in a well of self.
> None has a tear for others' woes
> Or cares what any other thinks.

The tragedy of human nature is that people do not always graduate from this preliminary period of selfishness, and out

[5] C. T. Craig, *The Beginning of Christianity* (New York and Nashville: Abingdon-Cokesbury Press, 1943), pp. 334-35.

41

of their own maladjustments they radiate unhappiness and trouble into their environments. They bar the coming of the Kingdom of God within their lives, and consequently mar its coming into society—a tiny mustard seed which might have grown into a tree to shelter the fowls of the earth is blighted by the evil of self-centeredness. The task of Jesus' religion is to get people away from this egocentricity. How different become the lives of people when they take seriously these admonitions of Jesus: "He that is greatest among you shall be your servant." "Let him . . . take up his cross, and follow me." "Whosoever shall lose his life . . . shall save it." Forgive "seventy times seven." "Be not anxious for your life." "Judge not, that ye be not judged." "Follow me." "Seek ye first the kingdom of God."

Rufus Jones has paraphrased the insights of Jesus in these words:

There are many fine people who never succeed in gaining inward peace. They are in a constant state of nerves, rushing about perplexed and weary, fussy and irritable. The trouble with these individuals is that they never succeed in forgetting themselves. Inward peace cannot come to a person who is always worrying about the results of his work, always wondering what other people will say about it, always showing touchiness about attention, recognition, and preferment. These are the very attitudes which frustrate peace, drive quietness from the heart.[6]

2. *Jesus' religion adjusts man to his fellow men*—the ethical aspect of religion. There is something compelling about the ethic of Jesus. A young girl remarked that "the Bible begins with Genesis and ends with 'Revolutions.'" She was poor in biblical scholarship but correct in the interpretation of the Christian ethic; Christianity does revolutionize one to go out and remake the world in which one lives! The oft-repeated stories of Kagawa, Grenfell, and Schweitzer are those of men whose lives were revolutionized by the Christian ethic; and

[6] Quoted by J. G. Gilkey, *God Will Help You* (New York: The Macmillan Co., 1943), p. 109.

I BELIEVE IN THE RELIGION OF JESUS

the number of people like them is legion. Caspar René Gregory is a classical example. In 1846 he was born in Philadelphia, Pennsylvania. He went to Germany for study, and there he remained to become a famous New Testament critic at Leipzig University. He tied Christian ethics mainly into the needs of the laboring man in Germany. One rainy night, they tell of him, he saw a streetcar switchman working in the chilly rain. Dr. Gregory went to the man and told him he would watch the switch while the switchman went into the cafe for a cup of hot coffee. When World War I came, Dr. Gregory—then sixty-eight—enlisted in the German army because he wanted to share the lot of the workingman. In 1916 Gregory was killed in France. Says Martin Dibelius, Caspar René Gregory "was indeed an illustration of the word: 'Greater love has no man than this, that a man lay down his life for his friends.' " [7] If the real ethic of Jesus gets hold of a man, sacrificial living for one's friends must be the result!

What was the real ethic of Jesus? Several answers come to us from contemporary Christian thinkers: (1) Some scientific humanists say that if Jesus were living today he would ally himself with their group, that Jesus' main purpose was in giving man a set of ethical principles to follow, and that if we today follow Jesus' ethical demands we can *build* the Kingdom of God. They feel that the world's main difficulty revolves about man's maladjustment with his environment; hence our panacea for the world's trouble is mainly that of improving man and remedying the sick spots of our environment. Man should give himself better education, diet, medical care; and at the same time man's environment should be improved by means of better working conditions, shorter working hours, improved tenement houses, ample playgrounds, and social settlement houses. These realistic improvements will better man's adjustment to society, which is mainly what Jesus meant by his Kingdom preaching. If men will try to live like Jesus and join Jesuslike movements for the improvement of

[7] *The Sermon on the Mount*, pp. 123-25.

society, then men can gradually build the Kingdom of God. Man has the potentialities for making this world like that which Jesus dreamed it might become. The main thing is that we treat each other ethically with the spirit of Christ! Even though the humanists' ideal is noble, I doubt if it is the *real* ethic of Jesus.

(2) At the right wing of interpretation of the Christian ethic is a group of thinkers—largely influenced by European pessimism—who say that the importance of Jesus is not his ethical teachings, nor his ideals for us, nor even his character; we are concerned with him only as one who was completely obedient to God's will. Jesus is basically of value to us as one who made the transcendent God known to the world, and only in so far as we emulate Jesus' submission to God has he value for us. When we are absolutely submissive to God by letting all pride creep from ourselves, then God can give us faith and make his will known to us. Such a pattern of thinking places man in a passive ethical state. This passive ethical state of man is vividly described by a European theologian in his words to Dean Sperry at the close of the Edinburgh Conference in 1937: "We have been speaking about the ethic of Jesus, through the medium of the Church, as the way to make the world the Kingdom of God. If the Kingdom of God ever comes, it will be *entirely* a gift of God. There is nothing which man can do about it." Such an attitude, however, sounds more like a misinterpretation of Paul's letter to the Romans than a paraphrasing of Jesus' ethical attitudes.

(3) Another school of Christian thinkers anticipates very soon the end of the world—we call them the "apocalyptists." They see the four horsemen of the Apocalypse—war, famine, death, and pestilence—riding across the world. Some of the adherents of this movement saw Adolf Hitler as the Antichrist, the beast whose number is 666. Christ will soon return to lead the forces of righteousness at the battle of Armageddon. Hence the ethic of Jesus has little for the improvement of this world; this world is to be destroyed as soon as it has descended to its worst—and then will come the New Jerusalem for faith-

44

I BELIEVE IN THE RELIGION OF JESUS

ful believers. Everything one may do to improve the social structure of the world but retards the battle of Armageddon and
the coming of the New Jerusalem. Maybe tomorrow will be
the end—who knows? Recently I heard one of these apocalyptic preachers on the radio; he signed off with this statement:
"Tomorrow I shall be on the air, unless Christ has come in
the air!" In such a state of religious living the prime affair
of every person is to keep himself faithful and loyal to Christ
until Christ returns, but the ethic of Jesus has no driving improvement of the world's social structure. His ethic is one for
keeping the individual holy and undefiled from the world. (I
have a personal feeling that Jesus would be much embarrassed
were he to be here and hear such "ethical" preaching in his
name!)

(4) The Christian ethic is a religious ethic. A person is
ethical toward his fellow men as a result of his proper relationship to God. Ethics is the result of religious experience.
Man adjusts himself to God through repentance and faith,
which means that he allows himself to become an instrument
of God's *agape* (redemptive love). It means first an absolute
surrender of self-will to the Overspirit (God) which surrounds
him. Second, it means an intellectual acceptance that God
is *agape*—as revealed in the New Testament—and that Jesus
Christ is both the incarnation of *agape* and the Messiah-Teach-
er who showed others how they might find the power of
agape in their own lives.

As I write at this moment in my study, an electric light
throws its reflective energy upon my desk, not by what the
globe and wires do by themselves, but by the energy they receive from a power plant to which they are related. Similarly
man does not possess *agape* merely by lifting himself by his
own bootstraps, but rather by his normal relationship to the
creative energy in the universe—God. "Emerson used to say
that if you hold a straw parallel to the Gulf Stream the ocean
will flow through the straw. It is true also that the moment
a life comes into parallelism with celestial currents [God's

45

energetic *agape*] the Divine will flow through it." [8] In such a way an individual becomes an instrument through which God's *agape* flows; the results are seen in his relationships with his fellow men.

The Sermon on the Mount gives to the ethical Christian a series of guideposts by which he can direct the channel of God's *agape* which flows through him. It guides a man to be merciful toward others; to love his enemies; to go the second mile—and the third—and the fourth; to pray for those who harmfully treat him; to forgive those who try to wrong him; to overcome evil with good; to refrain from censoriousness; to avoid anxiety. In every life situation the Christian acts with redemptive love (*agape*) toward his fellow men, since God creats him with *agape;* and if God's *agape* revolutionizes the life of a Christian believer, he becomes a natural medium through which God's *agape* flows into the organism called social reality. When God's *agape* can flow through all men as it transmitted itself through Jesus, then the Kingdom of God will have come to earth.

The question is often raised as to whether Jesus' ethic was an "interim ethic"—meant for Jesus' first-century followers for but a short time before the end of the present world— or an ethic for you and me today. Let us listen to three of the greatest contemporary New Testament scholars:

These commandments were given not for the short time intervening between the present and the end of the world. They were given for eternity, because they represent the will of the eternal God.—Martin Dibelius [9]

John the Baptist marks the dividing line. Before him, the law and the prophets; after him, the Kingdom of God. Any interim period is excluded. . . . There is a place for ethical teaching, not as "interim ethics," but as a moral ideal for men who have "ac-

[8] Rufus M. Jones, *The Radiant Life* (New York: The Macmillan Co., 1944), pp. 19-20.
[9] *The Sermon on the Mount*, p. 98.

46

cepted the Kingdom of God" and live their lives in the presence of His judgment and His grace, now decisively revealed.—CHARLES H. DODD [10]

The Kingdom is a process sprung from the fellowship of men with Jesus, and still more important from their fellowship with him and each other after his resurrection. . . . Through obedience unto faith, through following his guidance, through absorption of his spirit, through living his life. . . . That is the Gospel, as the New Testament understands it.—FREDERICK C. GRANT [11]

3. *Jesus' religion adjusts man to God.* It excites thoughtful men to believe in God and to worship him. Man cannot be satisfied to worship himself—bad psychological religion!—or even humanity—ethical but not good theology! He must worship something more than himself or he cannot bear the burden of himself. Bernard Shaw, sometimes smarty and cynical, said in a great and serious moment, "I tell you that as long as I can conceive something better than myself I cannot be easy unless I am striving to bring it into existence—or clearing the way for it." Jesus conceived the Kingdom of God as that "something better than myself" and he bade men to allow God's *agape* to flow through them so that God might work vitally in history. In this way could he give his Kingdom to men!

When man has repentance and faith—characterized by both intellectual belief and psychological trust—he has exemplified the "push" of the Christian religion. But there is the "pull" also, which is outside man and is identified with the energetic mercy (*agape*) of God. In nature we call this pull the fact of evolution, a cosmic urge, an *élan vital;* in religion we reverently call it "God." Dr. Halford E. Luccock was met one day by a student's remark, "Religion is all moonshine!" To which Dr. Luccock replied: "I agree. Have you ever been in Panama where the moonshine pulls up bil-

[10] *The Parables of the Kingdom* (New York: Charles Scribner's Sons, 1936), pp. 48, 109.
[11] "Form Criticism and the Christian Faith."

lions of tons of water at the time of a twenty-two-foot tide? The moonshine shows the pull of another world, unseen but resistless in force. Religion is like that; it is unseen but resistless in its pull upon the life of man!"

Isaiah felt the pull of God in the temple when he said, "I saw . . . the Lord . . . high and lifted up." Augustine understood this pull as he described it in his *Confessions,* "My heart is restless, O Lord, until it rests in thee." The mystic showed a keen insight into this upward urge as she told of her "flight of the alone to the Alone" where spirit touched Spirit. The gospel record expresses the constant pull of God in Christ as mediated on Jesus' lips, "And I, if I be lifted up . . . , will draw [pull] all men unto me."

Jesus has been the perennial pull for members of the Christian faith. A glance at his life has made men restless to live above the ordinary planes of existence; they have desired through repentance and faith to find the Kingdom about which he preached; they have desired to fashion their wills in harmony with God's will, as he so intricately did, that God's *agape* might flow through them into the needy stream of humanity. Through Christ's total insights into religion have men been pulled into their proper adjustment to God.

H. G. Wells said of Jesus, "He is too big for our small hearts." But it is this bigness of Jesus—and his vast comprehension of religion—which keeps him the constant pull for most of us, who echo the words of a twentieth-century mystic: "There are times when I feel like washing my hands of the whole concern of living. But there is always that strange man upon his cross who pulls me back again—and again—and again." [13]

Yes, I believe in religion in general, but more specifically I believe in the religion of Jesus! Interpreters in every age face "the peril of modernizing Jesus"; they encounter, however, the even greater danger of not catching up with his insights into life. The degree to which his "way of life" is woven into

[13] Paraphrased from the words of George Tyrrell to F. von Hügel.

individual and social experience determines the level upon which God's Kingdom has come into the world. Upon such a gesture of faith does the Christian venture his life! Occasionally a person who has followed Jesus' insights is able to say in the words of John Magee's sonnet:

> With silent, lifting mind I've trod
>   The high untrespassed sanctity of space,
>   Put out my hand and touched the face
> Of God.[13]

What more can one expect from religion?

[13] "Sunward I've Climbed."

I BELIEVE IN PRAYER

A LETTER RECEIVED RECENTLY FROM DR. GERALD HEARD SPEAKS OF A "college of prayer" on the Pacific Coast in which a particular study is being made by a group of people on one theme—prayer. Such an enterprise is tremendously intriguing; it makes one wish eagerly to be a student in such a "college"! Prayer for some people is an elective of life; in this "college" it is the subject of major concentration. Prayer is not one of the extracurricular experiences to be taken if one has the time; rather it is one of life's basic obligations, and the degree which one prays largely determines the healthful tone of one's life. One of the world's great contemporary students of prayer —shall we call him a postgraduate student?—is E. Stanley Jones. In his lucid booklet *How to Pray* he reminds us of this tonal value of prayer:

If I had one gift, and only one gift, to make to the Christian Church, I would offer the gift of prayer. Prayer tones up the total life. I find by actual experience I am better or worse as I pray more or less. If my prayer life sags, my whole life sags with it; if my prayer life goes up, my life as a whole goes up with it. To fail here is to fail all down the line; to succeed here is to succeed everywhere.

For the last eighteen months I have concentrated my study on the classical devotional writings of the Christian centuries. Among the contributors to the devotional life of the church I have discovered anew a "fellowship of the saints." I have met afresh Thomas à Kempis, Augustine, Francis of Assisi,

50

I BELIEVE IN PRAYER

John Woolman, Brother Lawrence; I have made a closer friendship of Dionysius the Areopagite, Lancelot Andrewes, Walter Hilton, Blessed Henry Suso; I have admired more deeply Teresa of Avila, Francis de Sales, William Law, John of the Cross. Although these men and women are of different backgrounds, from different countries, in different centuries, and facing different problems, they possess a common medium of expression—that of prayer. They are diverse in many ways, yet they speak a common language—the language of the Spirit, in which they learned how "to practice the presence of God." This "fellowship of the saints" has taught me a lesson never to be forgotten: either these saints were deluded men and women—and I do not believe that they were—or else many of us are missing "the feast of the Kingdom" which they so thoroughly enjoyed! Do we not satisfy our spiritual hunger too often with the crumbs from the spiritual table of God when we might, like the saints, richly participate in the spiritual banquet which God so willingly wants to give us?

Baron von Hügel told Rufus Jones that saints fulfilled four basic conditions of life:

He, or as is more often the case, *she*, must have been throughout life loyal to the Faith of the Church. . . . The person must have been heroic. . . . The person who is to rank as a saint must have been the recipient of powers beyond his ordinary human capacities. . . . He must, she must, have been radiant.[1]

1. Bernard Bosanquet once said, "A person can never be a whole unless he joins a Whole." It was his way of reiterating that a person can never be an integrated personality unless he is integrated with God and society—and this process of integration is intricately interwoven into the artistry of prayer. *The psychological-ethical values of prayer—which affect man and society—are deepened in a person's life by the intellectual view he holds of God and the universe in which he and God organically co-operate.* Brother Lawrence has called prayer

---

[1] Jones, *The Radiant Life*, pp. 4, 5.

"practicing the presence of God." Prayer is exactly such an experience. Let me explain: I think of God as the Life of the universe, the Spirit of the world, the Creative Energy—filled with *agape*, or redemptive love—which is alive in the universe. God's Spirit gives unity to the universe in the same way that my life gives unity to me. Every person and every particle in the universe is related to the Universal Life in the same way that every cell in my body is related to my life spirit. My body is an organism; the universe is an organism. The cells of my body have interaction with one another; every part of the universe has interaction with every other part. Why? Because the Life of God is related to everything in existence! This means that God's Spirit is not only in the natural world but also continually touches man's spirit—the kingdom of God is within you!—even though man may not be aware of this intimacy. Prayer is the highest way by which man becomes aware of the personal immanence of God's Spirit as the Great Companion. Prayer shows man how to "practice the presence of God."

2. *There are various ways by which a God of goodness, beauty, and truth may become consciously experienced in the life of man; prayer, however, leads man to the mountaintop of his spiritual adventure.* Through music, poetry, drama, rational reflection, friendships, merciful deeds toward our fellow men—as well as through prayer—can the presence of God be practiced. A girl coming from a symphony is described by a poet as being "a little taller than when she went"; an American theologian came into his first great awareness of God as he saw John Drinkwater's *Abraham Lincoln* enacted in a New York theater; Emily Dickinson views the appreciation of literature, especially poetry, as an experience which takes us "up" the mountain trail, when she says:

> There is no frigate like a book
> To take us lands away,
> Nor any coursers like a page
> Of prancing poetry.[2]

[2] *The Poems of Emily Dickinson,* ed. Martha Dickinson Bianchi and Alfred Leete Hampson. By permission of Little, Brown & Co.

52

I BELIEVE IN PRAYER

Beautiful experiences make us aware of a God of beauty! There are those—such as the scientists—who contemplate God through truth. God cannot be seen in the test tube or in the atom by the instruments of scientists, but occasionally a scientist in his work does emerge into a moment of religious exaltation. The astronomical physicist, as he looks a million light-years into the universe—6,000,000,000,000,000,000 miles— occasionally has the experience of the psalmist:

> When I consider thy heavens, the work of thy fingers,
> The moon and the stars, which thou hast ordained;
> What is man, that thou art mindful of him?
> And the son of man, that thou visitest him? [3]

The reverent scientist, as he contemplates the mystery of cellular life in his laboratory, sometimes feels with Walt Whitman that "a mouse is miracle enough to stagger sextillions of infidels." [4] The tiny cell and the vast universe bring to man at least an awesome awareness of God as a designer!

To others the "presence of God" is most deeply felt in acts of redemptive kindness among men. It is they who best understand Jesus' words, "Blessed are the merciful: for they shall obtain mercy." Several years ago a college student from a privileged home spent his Christmas vacation, not in the usual round of teas and dances, but in working in the December mail rush in the post office; and with his earnings he contributed to the Christmas needs of a poverty-stricken family in a tenement home. On the Christmas Eve when he delivered the money to the needy family and saw the deep gratitude behind the sincere tears of the recipients, he said, "Never was God nearer to me than on that night!"

Through these ways—beauty, truth, goodness—the practice of God's beauty, truth, and goodness is experienced. Yet through prayer is man's *highest* experience of God given and the trilogy of beauty, truth, and goodness amplified to its

[3] Psalm 8:3-4.
[4] "Song of Myself."

zenith. Prayer tones one in his total appreciation of the values in the universe. It is in prayer that "the gaze of God," as Nicholas of Cusa expresses it, is focused upon us and we most truly see ourselves as we most truly are in the presence of God. Rufus Jones has succinctly portrayed man's experience of God as similar to that of a person climbing Mount Everest:

At first there are many paths which gradually converge, and up to a certain point there are many ways of traveling [via beauty, truth, goodness], but at the very last for the final climb there is only one way up [via prayer]. . . . The mystic has been there, and he comes to tell us that beyond all conjectures and inferences about the reality of God is the consciousness of enjoying His presence.[5]

3. *There are three levels of prayer: prayer for oneself (personal); prayer for others (intercessory); prayer in which attention is fixed concentratedly on God (divine communion).* Gerald Heard classifies these three types of prayer as Low Prayer, Middle Prayer, and High Prayer, pointing out uniquely how each of these is interwoven into the definition of religion as given by Micah: "What doth the Lord require of thee, but to do justly [personal], and to love mercy [toward one's neighbor], and to walk humbly with thy God [divine attention]?" It is this third type of prayer which gives to man his highest center of reference, which results in man's showing mercy (*agape*) toward his fellow men. Says Dr. Heard:

Dealing justly is purely a matter of conduct, an act and an act which need have in it no generosity. But when we go on to loving mercy we are faced with a state of mind and it is directed toward something wider and more fundamental than an act. It is a root from which spring deeds much greater than justice. . . . And when we reach the humble walk with God there has to be quite a new type of attention. Then one must have become constantly aware of the Unseen and of one's dependence on it.[6]

[5] *Religious Foundations* (New York: The Macmillan Co., 1933), pp. 5, 10.
[6] *A Preface to Prayer* (New York: Harper & Bros., 1944), p. 30.

54

I BELIEVE IN PRAYER

What Gerald Heard says here is the very heart of the Christian pattern of religious-ethical living: the reason that we treat our fellow men with *agape* (redemptive love) is the result of our proper relationship to God; and when we have found God's *agape* via prayer imbued with faith, it becomes a revolutionary force in our life which drives us redemptively into society.

Prayer affects man's relationship to himself, his fellow men, and God. Prayer deals with laws affecting personal relationships, but in no way does prayer directly affect the laws of nature. Prayer is not a way of changing God's laws to meet man's particular needs. Rather it is the normal way by which man finds the unity of his spirit with God's Spirit so that he may become an instrument of God's creative energy and redemptive love. God is a law-abiding being; the natural laws of his universe are not to be altered by praying people. Sometimes this attitude toward a law-abiding universe is violated. For example, the *London Daily Mail*, April 15, 1940, had an article under the headline "Prayer and Answer," from which the following lines are taken:

> On March 23 the British people, led by the King and Queen, joined in a national day of prayer. In the seven days following . . . the German bombers were kept at home by bad weather conditions, and the people of this country had a record respite from air raids. . . . The weather in the Channel was entirely unsuitable for any enemy attempt at invasion.

There is a real danger in this kind of prayer interpretation. If the changed weather conditions were the result of prayer, what, then, can we say of Coventry, where the cathedral and vast numbers of townsfolk were destroyed on a night clear for bombing? Or how shall we interpret the impartial destruction of the people of an area devastated by a hurricane? Prayer does bring people courage, wisdom, power, and perspective for adventurous living if they can relate themselves to God's energy, love, and wisdom. It does not, however, change the weather or alter the laws of nature. Jesus realized this when he said God "sendeth rain on the just and on the unjust." Prayer did not save Jesus from Calvary; it did bring to him courage, selflessness, faith in God's righteousness as he made his climb to Calvary's summit!

4. *Prayer is an art which involves a careful technique: (1) preparation; (2) contemplation of God; (3) expectancy; (4) fruition.*

In the act of preparation we need to be *alone* with God—not necessarily physically alone (though it might greatly help), but spiritually alone:

> By all means use sometimes to be alone.
> Salute thyself; see what thy soul doth wear.
> Dare to look into thy chest; for 'tis thy own.[7]

In solitude the pray-er attains *quietude and calm*. Writes Emily Herman: "When we read the lives of the saints, we are struck by a certain large leisure which went hand in hand with a remarkable effectiveness. *They were never hurried.*"[8] The worshiper then feels his *humility*, or small creaturelike existence on this tiny planet, the kind Aldous Huxley describes in Philip Neri, "that specially 'modern' kind of humility which consists in having a sense of humor about oneself," which results in the worshiper's ceasing to worry about himself. Psychologically the attitudes of calm and humility breed *faith*, "a faith in Something Beyond us, enthusiasm for Something Above us that makes life worth living, that gets us out of our dead level, and sets us free to go on. . . . We must get out of the stage of worry into the stage of wonder; out of the stage of theory into the thrill of a love affair."[9]

In this kind of emerging experience our minds swing from self-preparation to contemplation and adoration of God; we have found a new center of reference in prayer!

[7] George Herbert.
[8] *Creative Prayer*, p. 31. Italics mine.
[9] Rufus Jones, *The Radiant Life*, p. 49.

I BELIEVE IN PRAYER

Out of this adoration and contemplation of an energetic, merciful God a mood of expectancy creeps into the pray-er. Prayer is not just autosuggestion—that is, a pep talk to oneself—but unless a person can pray sincerely with great expectation, God has a difficult time to answer prayer. If God is the Creative Energy of the universe, a praying person ought to expect added energy for his living, created out of his harmonious contact with God. Dr. Alexis Carrel says that "Prayer Is Power": "Prayer is . . . the most powerful form of energy that one can generate. . . . Its results can be measured in terms of increased physical buoyancy, greater intellectual vigor, moral stamina." [10] Also, out of worship a person should expect *a solution for a problem,* since God is a being of wisdom —maybe the person himself is the problem! Writes Dr. Henry Nelson Wieman about prayer and problem solving: "Private worship is doing two things: finding out what is wrong with oneself; and establishing that personal attitude through which one can receive from sources outside himself those influences which will correct the wrong which is in him." [11] When this expectancy of problem solving is harnessed with the energy received in worship, there arises in the spirit of the worshiper an expectancy of *redemptive use of himself in society,* just as God's energy and *agape* have been used so freely by him. I think that this was the way Jesus expected God's reign to come among men: it would start within—and then out of transfigured worshipers it would radiate to society.

The manner by which the praying person lives in society is the fruitive aspect of worship—"By their fruits ye shall know them." The result of worship is seen as a well-integrated individual leaves the sanctuary to transform his environment. Dr. Reinhold Niebuhr well illustrated the fruitive value of worship when he said in the dedicatory service of the Rockefeller Memorial Chapel at the University of Chicago: "A

[10] *Reader's Digest,* March, 1941.

[11] *Methods of Private Religious Living* (New York: The Macmillan Co., 1929), pp. 26-27.

CREDO—FUNDAMENTAL CHRISTIAN BELIEFS

beautiful chapel has been erected for our worship. The test of its worship-value will be found in the way by which we leave its doors to go out and create a beautiful world!"

If prayer is truly fruitive, it will transform each of us—and as renewed, rededicated people we then create a new world. Listen again to Dr. Alexis Carrel:

> Today, as never before, prayer is a binding necessity in the lives of men and nations. The lack of emphasis on the religious sense has brought the world to the edge of destruction. Our deepest source of power and perfection has been left miserably undeveloped. Prayer, the basic exercise of the spirit, must be actively practiced in our private lives. The neglected soul of man must be made strong enough to assert itself once more. For if the power of prayer is again released and used in the lives of common men and women; if the spirit declares its aims clearly and boldly, there is yet hope that our prayers for a better world will be answered.[12]

Comments Douglas Steere on this curative value of prayer as seen through the eyes of Dostoevski:

> There is a profound insight here that we are each in a mysterious way bound unto a responsibility for all the sin in the world. Dostoevski has depicted this for us with a prophetic vividness.
> Yet, Dostoevski, as a devout Christian, pointed men to inward identification with the redeeming love of God, prompt and active through a Christ who will not cease to travail until He has won from within each man a response to Him, and an eagerness to live in a brotherly love that rises and is sustained out of this common life with Him. According to Dostoevski, this revolution is going on now. It begins within. It can begin with you and with me, and with my neighbor.[18]

And go out into the wide recesses of the world!
  Let us pray.

[12] *Op. cit.*
[18] *On Beginning from Within* (New York: Harper & Bros., 1943), p. xii.

58

I BELIEVE IN THE ROLE OF THE
CHURCH AND ITS MEMBERS

THE SETTING IS EPHESUS IN ASIA MINOR; THE YEAR IS A.D. 55. A converted rabbi, Paul, described as one who looks sometimes "like a man and sometimes like an angel," is writing to his friends at Corinth. In a high moment he speaks of the Church as "the body of. Christ," an organism in which the members have various functions to perform as do various members of the human body; and then in the height of his inspired Christian perspective he merges into his "Hymn to *Agape*" (I Cor. 13), saying that the final test of a church member's status is the degree of redemptive love (*agape*) he possesses. Nineteen centuries later, in the summer of 1937, 550 delegates from forty countries meet at Oxford, England, and Edinburgh, Scotland; in their ecumenical meetings Paul's idea sets the general basis for their concept of the Church. The basic idea of the Church held by the first-century apostle has not been outmoded by the changing centuries!

The most encouraging note in the chaos of the present historical moment is that the Church is organized on a world-community basis at a time when hatred and warfare have ridden rampant across civilization. Fortunately, when the distressing conference at Munich came in 1938, it had been preceded in 1937 by the ecumenical conferences of the Church at Oxford and Edinburgh. If there is any world institution able to direct the hopes of men to some ideal for civilization at this moment of international catastrophe, it is the Christian Church.

CREDO—FUNDAMENTAL CHRISTIAN BELIEFS

Many individuals, earlier indifferent toward the Church, see it now as the one world institution in which to place faith for tomorrow's world. Albert Einstein's words represent the feelings of many people today:

Being a lover of freedom, when the revolution came in Germany, I looked to the universities to defend it, knowing that they had always boasted of their devotion to the cause of truth; but, no, the universities immediately were silenced. Then I looked to the great editors of the newspapers whose flaming editorials in days gone by had proclaimed their love of freedom; but they, like the universities, were silenced in a few short weeks. . . . Only the Church stood squarely across the path of Hitler's campaign for suppressing truth. I never had any special interest in the Church before, but now I feel a great affection and admiration because the Church alone has had the courage and persistence to stand for intellectual truth and moral freedom. I am forced thus to confess that what I once despised I now praise unreservedly.

The role of the Church as the world's guide will be difficult because at a time when we do think of a unified world church, national barriers are terrifically severe; when we do hope for world concord and amity, the note of divisiveness and world strife is internationally ingrained; when we in the Church do try to put spiritual things first, it happens to be a time in history when materialism is woven intricately into the fabric of the contemporary world. Yet like Augustine in the fifth century, who saw the "city of man" in the throes of destruction but was able to envision the "City of God" for the future, we today see the Church as the custodian of ultimate values which keeps pointing us to a better world on the morrow!

1. *The Church is a body of believers.* What does that phrase mean? A believer is one who has faith: and if a person has faith, he believes something about God and Christ (the intellectual aspect); he trusts God completely by letting himself become an instrument of God's will (the psychological aspect);

60

he becomes something and does something in the world where he lives (the ethical aspect).

As the Christian works out his intellectual beliefs about God and Christ, he realizes that the ethical standards of Christianity do not vary greatly from those of other great religions. Christianity, however, is unique among world religions in its stressing of redemptive love (*agape*) as one of God's prime qualities—a type of love which *gives* itself to the unattractive, the undeserving, the unlovely, the lonely, the lost. It is a love which God gives to men in order that he may remedy and supplement the weakness and frailty of human beings, and the believer initially makes himself open to this love through his intellectual receptivity. This *agape* is not something passive in the universe; the Christian believes that God is a being of majesty and power; he is the Creative Energy, the vibrant Life of the Universe, a God of tremendous greatness! This the Christian believes about God; and he also believes that Jesus Christ became the complete embodiment of God's *agape* —he was full of mercy (*agape*) and truth!

As a Christian believer holds these intellectual concepts about God, he then says, "I shall surrender my spirit to God's Spirit. I shall be absolutely obedient to God's will. I want myself to become a perfect instrument of God's *agape!*" Through these intellectual and psychological aspects of faith the believer adjusts his life to the Life of God, and the tests of his adjustment to God's *agape* are seen in the ways by which he adjusts himself via *agape* to his fellow men. He sees the ethical code of Christianity, the Sermon on the Mount, not as a set of moral rules to be kept, but as a series of "guideposts" by which he can direct himself as an instrument of God's redemptive love in relation to his fellow men. These guideposts portray one who has *agape* as poor in spirit, meek, merciful, humble; he overcomes evil with good, goes the second mile, is free of anxiety, loves his enemies and prays for his persecutors, is not censorious, is concerned with character rather than reputation, builds his life upon the solid reality of God.

61

Paul spoke of the various members of "the body of Christ" with diverse tasks to do—some were apostles, some were prophets, some were teachers, some were miracle workers; but all were to be instruments of God's *agape,* else they were as a "tinkling cymbal" or "sounding brass." And so the pattern for membership in this "body" today is the same. We are people differently composed of reason, feeling, biological heritages, environmental influences. Some of us are called to be musicians, some to be scientists, some to be political leaders, some to be business executives, some to be ministers, some to be teachers; yet all of us as "the body of Christ" are emissaries of God's *agape* in our communities. The way in which men spread redemptive love into the lives of their fellow men portrays their adjustment to society; this adjustment to society is really the test of their adjustment to God.

2. *How are members of the Church related to the community?* Today we Christians speak of the desire for world fellowship and world peace, yet in our smaller communities we must live this fellowship and promote this peace if we are sincerely practicing *agape*. It is sometimes easier to speak theoretically about world brotherhood than to practice that theory in our smaller areas of experience. Several years ago, when the Nazis were persecuting the Jews in Germany, the members of a ministerial conference sent a cablegram to Adolf Hitler in protest of the maltreatment of Jews. The minister who reported this incident to *The Christian Century* said that he was thoroughly in favor of sending the cablegram to Hitler, but felt that perhaps some of the men who signed the cablegram were a bit more concerned with the way Hitler was treating the Jews in Germany than they were as to how some of their parishioners were treating Negroes in America. This dilemma between theory and practice the Christian believer tries to avoid.

If the Church is to be effective in the smaller community, it must first aid the individual—who is a "cell" in the organism called the Church—to become integrated to himself. The Church through worship service and pastoral care can minister to the mental-spiritual torment. Half of our hospital beds are used by people who are mentally, not physically, ill; 50 to 75 per cent of the patients who come into doctors' offices are mentally, not organically, sick and need a pastor more than a medical doctor; one out of fourteen people in a metropolitan state like New York visits a mental hospital or clinic at some time. Facts like these arouse us to the Church's problem in helping these people become adjusted to themselves.

If worship and pastoral care can direct man's center of reference to God and show how man can become a believer, intellectually and psychologically, then the Church has done its first task in helping the devotee become adjusted to God and to himself. Furthermore, the believer will have found that Christianity as a religion brings energy, joy, and unselfishness to him, that it is something which supports and defends him in each life situation.

The test of the worship service and the pastoral aid of the Church does not end when it has brought mental health to the individual. Mental health cannot be retained by an individual unless he serves others. If the Church plays its role for the individual, it stimulates the worshiper to practice *agape* in his community. He leaves the sanctuary filled with *agape*, hoping that he can spread redemptive love to the unfortunate, the lost, the unredeemed, the lonely in his community. The areas where he may extend *agape* in any community in the United States are many; several areas will suffice for illustration:

(1) The Negro problem is one of the most turbulent in American life today; it is a virgin field for many believers to practice *agape*. The tragic fact of being a Negro in America was shown recently by a Negro girl who won a prize in an essay contest: "How Should We Punish Adolf Hitler?" She said that the worst punishment would be to give him a black skin and force him to live in the United States the rest of his life! In a country which sees all men as equal in privilege we need deep repentance for our treatment of the Negroes. In

63

eleven southern states we spend an average of $44.00 per white student in the public schools, only $12.50 on each Negro student; we have one hospital bed for each 150 white people, but one hospital bed for each 2,000 Negroes—among whom sickness status and death rate are worse than among white people.

Booker T. Washington has set us an example of *agape*. One day when he arrived at a town for an address, the white cab driver refused to drive him to the auditorium. Mr. Washington said to the driver, "All right, then. You get in the rider's seat, and I'll drive you to the auditorium!" Do not many of us so-called believers need to mimic the humility and *agape* of Booker T. Washington as we try to relieve the misery of the Negroes?

(2) Another area where believers can show redemptive love in the smaller communities is in the realm of juvenile delinquency.

A modern poet saw that privileged people do not always show *agape* toward youth who come from less fortunate homes. She wrote these lines:

> The golf links lie so near the mill
> That almost every day
> The laboring children can look out
> And see the men at play.[1]

Christian believers see responsibility going hand in hand with privilege. Thus they try to make Christian settings for youth, but they also try to make Christian youth for those settings.

(3) Both employers and employees in the Church will try to settle their problems with one another with redemptive love. And what a problem this realm offers to believers in America! In 1929—the last year of "prosperity"!—85 per cent of the people in the United States had too low a standard of

[1] Sarah N. Cleghorn, "The Golf Links Lie So Near the Mill," *Portraits and Protests* (New York: Henry Holt & Co., 1917).

64

living, according to government statistics. The Heller budget now asks for a $2,900 a year minimum family income for health and decency; yet today, amid our economic boom, 70 per cent of the citizens of this country receive less than $2,000 a year!

Christian employers and employees need imagination to put themselves in each other's positions, and then with *agape* go out as servants to alleviate the difficulties that keep them divided. Sir William Beveridge of the London School of Economics has given this suggestion: "Strikes and lockouts and other industrial stoppages could be put to an end pretty quickly if employers and employees would try to put themselves in thought and imagination in each other's places, and see the various questions at issue from each other's point of view." Especially if they would see the issues involved through Christian eyes!

The Malvern Conference, meeting in January, 1941, in England, expressed the necessity for the Christian community to possess proper economic standards. Its statement concluded:

We believe that the most vital demands to be made by the church with a view to social reconstruction are two: The restoration of man's economic activity to its proper place as the servant of his whole personal life; and the expression of his status in the natural world as a child of God for whom Christ died.

(4) The Christian believer realizes that the Church will never be a body of people possessing *agape* so long as there are frictions between Jews, Catholics, and Protestants. He will try to heal difficulties between these groups with redemptive love.

A Christian symbol of interfaith and interracial unity was beautifully portrayed at a Good Friday service, 1939, in Washington, D. C., as Marian Anderson sang "Ave Maria" standing by the Lincoln memorial. There stood a Negro Protestant woman singing a Roman Catholic aria in praise of a Jewish woman, Mary, the mother of Jesus. That is a memorable portrait of *agape* being practiced in America!

3. How are members of the Church related to the state? Our national hymn "America" ends with the suggestion that we as American Christians have a double devotion to church and state:

> Protect us by thy might,
> Great God our King.

A Christian needs to have a bifocal vision when it comes to his loyalties to the Church and to his government. The Church is an institution which uses *agape* as the ultimate way to solve problems; the state is an institution which may resort to force to solve her difficulties. As citizens of both, church members often find themselves in a dilemma. War illustrates this. Some become conscientious objectors in order that they may be absolutely true to the way of redemptive love. Others follow the dictate of the Oxford Conference: "It is our [Christians'] duty to do what is relatively best." They feel that the "relatively best" in an age of terrorism is fighting a foe. They believe that it is better to use the sword and remain free men than to be conquered by the enemy and become slaves; for they reason that with the conquest of this country by the enemy all good institutions—including the Church—would be destroyed. Thus they envision force as a momentary expedient to save the Church as well as the nation, yet they continue to believe that the Church as the custodian of *agape* points to the final way by which men and women must live together!

Aldous Huxley has reminded us that unless we are careful we may lose the tone of love in our civilization. We become calloused to love as we see at the movies, hear on the radio, and read in the magazines the continuous note of hate and killing. It is a danger that modern man confronts; and it is the task of the Church and its members to remind civilization continuously that *"agape* never passes away," because God is *agape*. And because God is *agape* and is not to be defeated, those who are believers have faith that redemptive

66

love must finally be the way by which all people live together on this planet. This ideal of *agape* which the Church keeps alive is like a star—it is something which we cannot presently touch, even though we reach for it, but it guides us to our

love must finally be the way by which all people live together on this planet. This ideal of *agape* which the Church keeps alive is like a star—it is something which we cannot presently touch, even though we reach for it, but it guides us to our destiny even though the path at our feet seems dark.

4. *How are members of the Church related to the world?* I remember as a small boy hearing my elders say of the Russo-Japanese War, "It is so far away that it has no concern for us in the United States, especially in Iowa." That was in 1904. Today, in 1945, the world has vastly changed. A conflict anywhere affects the entire populace on this planet. In such an age, when most great secular problems are world problems, there is a tremendous necessity that some ideal way or institution be big enough to influence the solution of such problems. The Ecumenical Church with her world consciousness assumes that role!

Paul said that the Church is "the body of Christ." The ecumenical movement has made that body a world organism. Each believer is a cell in a local church; and each local church is bound up with others in the community, the state, the nation as a part of the total organism—the Body of Christ—the World Church.

Today there are 650,000,000 Christians in the world. May those members attempt to save civilization by living lives of redemptive love! On these members as the Body of Christ civilization depends.

I BELIEVE IN A FRIENDLY UNIVERSE

SOMEONE HAS SUGGESTED THAT THE FIGURE IN RODIN'S "THE Thinker" was contemplating the question, Is the universe friendly? It is possible that this is a correct assumption, because that is the ultimate question for which most people and religions seek an answer. The experience of J. Middleton Murry in pondering this problem is similar to our own. After World War I he found himself in a state of morbidity—depressed, lonely, afraid. His universe seemed hostile to him. Listen to his words: "I had come to the end of my tether. I had reached a point of total dereliction and despair. It was 'irrecoverably dark, total eclipse.'" Many of his friends had been killed in France; others had been maimed and gassed; most were having a difficult time in making postwar adjustments. His life was so torn within that he contemplated suicide in Trafalgar Square. And then his famous wife, Katherine Mansfield, the writer, died. This sent Middleton Murry into seclusion, with the hope that he might see the problem of his life in better perspective. This is what happened in his solitude:

A moment came when the darkness of that ocean changed to light, the cold to warmth; when it swept in one great wave over the shores and the frontier of myself, when it bathed me and I was renewed; when the room was filled with a Presence, and I knew that I was not alone, that I never could be alone any more; that the universe beyond held no menace, for I was a part of it; that in some way for which I had sought in vain so many years, I belonged; and because I belonged I was no longer I, but some-

I BELIEVE IN A FRIENDLY UNIVERSE

thing different, which could never be afraid in the old ways or cowardly with the old cowardice.[1]

1. *The universe seems unfriendly to some because they look at life with indifference and cynicism.* They are bewildered about the whole problem of living, with wars and financial depressions added to the usual gamut of perplexities. In their confusion they know not what to believe, and with Sara Teasdale they are willing to echo:

> One by one, like leaves from a tree,
> All my faiths have forsaken me.[2]

They see warring, grasping men as less co-operative than ants, beavers, or bees. They read Ecclesiastes and chime with it about life, "Vanity of vanities; all is vanity." They read Spengler's *Decline of the West* and feel that all historical eras are determined in cycles, but they fail to read Sorokin's *Crisis of Our Age,* which sees the possibility of an "ideational" period of history merging from the last six hundred years of "sensate" living. They pick up Pitkin's *Life Begins at Forty,* hoping to be encouraged that at least in middle age life may hold purpose for them, only to read in Sheldon's *Prometheus Unbound* that "the human mind at forty is commonly vulgar, smug, deadened, and wastes its hours. There are few who go on toward mental growth."

The man who faces life with this "will toward cynicism" will never get beyond a feeling that the universe is indifferent and unfriendly, that life is

> a tale
> Told by an idiot, full of sound and fury,
> Signifying nothing.

What T. R. Glover once said of Marcus Aurelius, "He does not believe enough to be great," I would repeat about those

[1] Quoted by W. L. Stidger, *Men of the Great Redemption* (Nashville: Cokesbury Press, 1931), pp. 164-65.
[2] "Leaves."

69

who in their cynicism call the universe unfriendly. Their real problem lies within themselves rather than outside in the structure of the universe.

2. *Tragedy—or beyond tragedy?* This question every man asks of his experiences, as he delves more deeply into the problem of a friendly universe. "Every real tragedy," says Joseph Wood Krutch, "however tremendous it may be, is an affirmation of faith in life, a declaration that even if God is not in his Heaven, then at least Man is in his world. . . . For the great ages tragedy is not an expression of despair but the means by which they saved themselves from it." [3] For those who accept this "stoical" view of evil, the universe, indifferent to man, is as unfriendly as man allows it to be. The real problem of suffering lies within man himself, rather than in the structure of the universe.

William Ernest Henley, facing suffering through a series of surgical operations, shows the innate courage of man when he says:

> It matters not how strait the gate,
>   How charged with punishments the scroll,
> I am the master of my fate:
>   I am the captain of my soul.[4]

Undoubtedly many are saved from cynicism and despair of an unfriendly universe by such a "will to live"—especially when they are in their virile, creative years—but I feel in agreement with William James that "old age has the last word: the purely naturalistic look at life [like Krutch's and Henley's], however enthusiastically it may begin, is sure to end in sadness. This sadness lies at the heart of every merely positivistic, agnostic, or naturalistic scheme of philosophy." [5] The average mature man in facing life's struggles is not al-

[3] *The Modern Temper* (New York: Harcourt, Brace & Co., 1929), pp. 125, 126.
[4] "Invictus."
[5] *The Varieties of Religious Experience*, p. 140.

ways satisfied merely to say, "Well, at least we have one another."

Real tragedy asks man to have self-reliance, to trust himself—certainly a dignified step beyond cynicism. Christianity, on the other hand, peers "beyond tragedy," asking that man center his trust in the Life of the Universe, whose organic life is a God of energy and redemptive love. The tragic hero's world is as big as the individual himself, and may break in two when frustrations come which are too great for a human being to shoulder. The Christian's world is as big as God himself and can never break in two, for "*agape* [the Spirit of an eternal God] never passes away." Christianity believes in a universe that is friendly because it believes in a God of redemptive love!

In comparing tragedy and Christianity, James W. Dabbs writes:

One goes from tragedy to Christianity, and it is but a step; but it is not an easy step. . . . It is a difficult step because it is a step from pride to humility. The tragic hero is self-relying; too self-relying; proud in his self-reliance. This is his strength and, as the Greeks were aware, this is his weakness. The step is possible, however, because of the common mood of pity. Life is pitiful in both the tragic and the Christian view, but in different ways: it is more purely pitiful in Christianity; in tragedy pity is balanced by fear.[6]

And might we not add that in Christianity "*agape* casteth out fear!"

In tragedy man trusts himself; in Christianity man trusts God. Often when the tragic hero finds his suffering too great he reaches for his sword—as did Othello. When the Christian finds his suffering beyond human endurance he reaches out with faith in God and cries, "Father, into thy hands I commend my spirit"—as did Jesus. The Christian dies, not in despair of a cold or indifferent universe, rather with a trust in a friendly universe whose life is God.

[6] "Beyond Tragedy," *Christendom*, Spring, 1936.

71

The Christian never looks at life through easy eyes; he sees the shadow of the cross in every circumstance of human experience. The cross, written into reality, symbolizes that God as the Great Companion and Overspirit works and suffers with him in every life situation. God is more than a spectator of man in his struggles—he is a participant! Out of the realization of this divine-human partnership the Christian can say with a melioristic, rugged hope, "All things work together for good to them that love God." Man and God may have a long struggle laboring together for God's plan for humanity on this planet; but the Christian never despairs of the future, for his faith discerns God's hand in control of the final outcome of history.

3. *If the universe is friendly, what, then, is God doing about the problem of suffering?* Suffering in man's experiences falls under one of two possibilities: (1) events which he in no way has caused, illustrated by the cyclone, the tornado, the drought (physical evil); (2) circumstances in which he has played a role through misuse of freedom, illustrated by wars, depressions, and the daily little evils, such as suspicion, hatred, jealousy, fear, which lay waste life (moral evil). About all these events which distort man there is a double query: (1) Why do they happen? and (2) Since they are here, what is God doing about them?

Maude Royden once said, "I have no absolute solution for the problem of suffering, but I have always found that when I reach out for help I find Something in my universe to help me face suffering." Many feel this way especially about the problem of physical evil; it seems an insoluble problem; it is an enigma which brings distortion to "the just and the unjust" alike. Some like Edgar S. Brightman believe:

There is in God's very nature something which makes the effort and pain of life necessary. . . . The evils of life and the delays in the attainment of value, in so far as they come from God and not from human freedom, are thus due to his nature, yet not wholly to his deliberate choice. . . . This element we call The

72

I BELIEVE IN A FRIENDLY UNIVERSE

Given. . . . The Given is the source of an eternal problem and task for God.[7]

Brightman sees "The Given" as a spur to God's activity to help man, just as suffering among our fellows stimulates us to help them in their troubles. The Given limits only God's *momentary* power, so that he cannot stop the cyclone, the tornado, the drought; but The Given does not retard God's perfect wisdom and supreme goodness, nor does The Given thwart God from using men's mistakes and sufferings for his ultimate purpose for them upon this planet. The Given "places the Cross in the eternal nature of God," but it gives to man a God worthy of love and worship. While Brightman's attempt to solve the problem of physical evil may not be satisfactory for some—they feel that it is too metaphysical and highly speculative—it is at least an honest, rugged suggestion for the problem of physical suffering in a law-abiding universe. It reminds us of this axiom: *God does not change the physical laws of the universe, because he cannot, since he abides by his own natural laws. God does, however, change human beings into courageous, purposive, sympathetic persons who help him alter the results of evil circumstance into a Beloved Community.*

Wartime always emphasizes the problem of suffering. It causes people to ask, "Why does God allow wars? Why doesn't God do something about wars like the present holocaust?" The Christian theist answers: God allows wars because he allows man to have free will. If in an unplanned, acquisitive society we sow the seeds of selfishness and nationalism, then we reap wars; "for whatsoever a man soweth, that shall he also reap." If, on the other hand, men live with the spirit of redemptive love toward one another and toward nations, then they shall reap a Beloved Community; but men in all great nations must realize this truth before it can become a working possibility for the world. This is a moral universe in which laws affecting personal relations are no more

[7] *The Problem of God* (New York: Abingdon Press, 1930), pp. 113, 183.

73

to be tampered with than the laws affecting the physical universe. The law of gravitation cannot be broken, only illustrated, by one who jumps from a ten-story building; in similar fashion the Christian law of human brotherhood necessarily built upon *agape* cannot be broken, only illustrated, by men and nations who build their structures upon the lust for material power.

What is God doing about the present war? The Christian theist believes that he is doing at least three things: (1) He is holding the moral structure of his universe together; the harvest time has come, so that we are reaping from the seeds we have sown in history. (2) He is suffering with man in this present turbulence, helping each righteous man in every life-situation, giving his energy and mercy and wisdom to those who turn to him for help in their time of trouble. (3) He is using the mistakes and the heartaches of the present chaos for some future good, employing those who seek his will as his emissaries for some future betterment of the world. After the conquests of Alexander the Great in the fourth century before the Christian era the process of Hellenizing the Mediterranean world was begun. It was fought tenaciously as a demonic influence in non-Greek cultures. But that which seemed for the moment an evil turned out to be a good in the first century of the Christian era. Paul was able through the common vehicle of the Greek language to spread Christianity throughout the Mediterranean world from Antioch in Syria to Rome in Italy. The Christian theist believes that, now as then, God will in some way with those who seek to do his will utilize the present sufferings for some future purposive good. Do not China, India, the isles of the Pacific suggest settings where present suffering may blossom into future good?

4. *What practical suggestions may I employ in order that I may grow into a deeper appreciation of a friendly universe?* Five possible helps I wish to mention: (1) Eustace Haydon says that evil "is no longer a metaphysical problem." [8] He sug-

[8] *The Quest of the Ages*, p. 140.

74

gests that much of man's suffering is due to his maladjustment to his environment, that the cure for this maladjustment lies largely in applying panaceas from science to both man and his environment. Give man better education, diet, housing, medical aid; improve his environment by sanitation, shorter hours, playgrounds and recreational centers, improved factory conditions, regulated supply and demand of economic goods—then you will give man an improved adjustment to his environment, which will greatly reduce the problem of suffering. This may not completely solve the problem of suffering—and I still hold to its metaphysical implications—but at least it is a necessary step toward any person's appreciation of a friendly universe that he do everything practical toward self-improvement.

(2) Let us admit that there is "the dark night of the soul" for many of us, just as there was for St. John of the Cross, when our viewpoints seem distorted and imbued with a mysterious melancholia. Listen to two men as diverse in time and ability as Martin Luther and Robert Louis Stevenson. Said Luther, "I am utterly weary of life. I pray the Lord will come forthwith and carry me hence. . . . Rather than live forty years more, I would give up my chance of Paradise." Wrote Stevenson, "There is indeed one element in human destiny that not blindness itself can controvert. Whatever else we are intended to do, we are not intended to succeed; failure is the fate allotted." [9] These dark moments occur in the experiences of most people; and when they come the universe seems, if not unfriendly, at least indifferent. The best curative for these occurrences is to analyze what is wrong, what can be corrected, then follow out the lines of clearest suggestion. A disciplining of oneself to a creative pattern of worship is often a curative for such states of despondency.

(3) Remember that a religious-philosophical viewpoint is one of a person's most precious possessions. There is in all

[9] Quoted by William James, *The Varieties of Religious Experience*, pp. 137-38.

of us "a will to live" but there is at the same time "a will to believe." It is easy to let a religious-philosophical structure slip into a shoddy negativity; it is just as easy to build this structure into a strong, supporting pattern if one has the will to believe. The experience of Carlyle illustrates what I mean. In his earlier years he looked out upon his universe as "a cold, inexhaustible steam engine"; the result in his life was one of fear. Later he said, "When I saw my universe as the living garment of a living God I was no longer afraid; I had courage."

(4) Many people are inwardly unhappy and in their unhappiness imagine an unfriendly universe; the solution of their problem is to lose themselves into something bigger than themselves. They suffer from psychological (imaginary) not logical fears. Those who are distorted by a state of psychological fear need to realize how basic worry is in creating such a state of mind. They would do well to emulate the woman who realized that worry was her chief means of coloring the universe into a state of unfriendliness and so made for herself a "worry table." In tabulating her worries she discovered that 40 per cent of them probably would never happen, her anxiety being the result of a tired mind; that 30 per cent of them were over old decisions which she could not alter, try as she might; that 12 per cent of them were about others' criticisms of her, most of them untrue and made by people who felt inferior to her; that 10 per cent of them concerned her health, which she knew would become worse the more she worried; that only 8 per cent of her worries were "legitimate"—and these "legitimate" worries were the types of experiences which when faced with her own resources, the help of friends, and the help of God, not only *taught* her something but *made* her something as well. Hence through her alleviation of worry she found one approach to a friendly universe.

(5) The Christian theist looks upon evil as real but purposive, because he believes in a friendly, merciful God who is real and purposive in his life. The Christian theist realizes

that the problem of suffering is an enigma, that he does not have all the answers for it; but he still trusts in God. Like Habakkuk he sits upon his watchtower and waits for further light, saying, "The righteous [man] lives by reason of his faithfulness." Or with James Russell Lowell he finds in his soul the echo:

Though the cause of Evil prosper, yet 't is Truth alone is strong. . . .
Truth forever on the scaffold, Wrong forever on the throne,—
Yet that scaffold sways the future, and, behind the dim unknown,
Standeth God within the shadow, keeping watch above his own.[10]

I cannot think easily about the problem of suffering; but because I believe in a God of *agape,* with Habakkuk and Lowell I cannot believe in an unfriendly universe.

[10] "The Present Crisis."

I BELIEVE THE CONTEMPLATION
OF DEATH ENRICHES LIFE

It is winter, 1945. I am sitting in my office, thinking about death—particularly *my* death. It brings me no sense of morbidity as I realize that my span of life on this planet will probably terminate in twenty-five years. Rather it gives to me a drive to do the worth-while things I want done . . . an incentive to be more kind and helpful to the people I meet . . . an impetus to live *this day* as though it were the last and best day of my existence. . . . Outside it is snowing. . . . The snow flakes are falling patiently and kindly, lodging securely on the boughs of the campus trees. . . . Through the soft snow curtain I discern the spire of the college chapel pointing upward as though to direct my thoughts to God. . . . The sight of the chapel reminds me of the 1,600 students who have walked in and out of its doors, now on the fighting fronts of the world. . . . I realize that death to many of them at this very moment is imminent. . . . I try to parallel their thoughts of death with mine. . . . I conclude that many of them are weighing death in possible terms of moments, hours, days; I am weighing my death in terms of years. That is the difference. I want to live my life as courageously and dynamically in the years that lie ahead as they are forced under the expediency of war to live their lives in these tragic days. . . . The thought of death deepens my desire to live!

As I ponder the fact of my death, and what it means to me, I guide my thoughts through the words of the Spanish thinker Unamuno:

I BELIEVE CONTEMPLATION OF DEATH ENRICHES

Although this meditation upon mortality may soon induce in us a sense of anguish, it fortifies us in the end. Retire, reader, into yourself and imagine a slow dissolution of yourself—the light dimming about you, all things becoming dumb and soundless, enveloping you in silence, the objects that you handle crumbling away between your hands, the ground slipping from under your feet, your very memory vanishing as if in a swoon, everything melting away from you into nothingness and you yourself also melting away, the very consciousness of nothingness, merely as the phantom harbourage of a shadow, not even remaining to you.[1]

I arise from my chair and say to myself, "I am not afraid of death; I believe that death is necessary in order to enrich life!"

1. *Death is a part of the totality of experience; it is never to be isolated as something separate from life; it is synonymous with selfless living.* Said Jesus, "Whosoever shall lose his life . . . shall save it." Such a dictum is a part of every man's experience in this temporal span of experience; it is likewise an insight into that moment when every man adventurously steps from a space-time world into the realm of eternal events. In his daily living the Christian learns how to die. Said Paul, "I die daily." There is a bundle of selfish desires within each person from which he must graduate before he can appreciate the experience of being "resurrected" to a higher kind of living. If it is the native purpose of a child to be selfish until he is eight years of age, it is the sacred task of a maturing person to "die daily" to his egocentricity.

Two contemporary writers vivify this shift which must be made in the process of living if one is to learn the art of dying in order to obtain worth-while living. One writer describes a woman called Edith who was "a little country bounded on the north, south, east, and west—by Edith." Edith was a selfish individual who never had graduated from childish egocentricity. The other novelist has one of her characters—a girl struggling to keep her values—say, "Life's just

[1] *Tragic Sense of Life* (New York: The Macmillan Co., 1921), p. 42.

too much trouble unless one can live for something big!" It is this dying from the type of Edith-self and living to the type patterned by the girl who will live for something big which is at the heart of Christian experience. To "die daily" to selfish living is necessary if life is to be enriched according to the Christian pattern; it is the avenue to the resurrected life of *agape.*

Voltaire poignantly illustrates what I mean. In his earlier years, before he had established a constructive viewpoint of life, he said, "I hate to live, and yet I am afraid to die." In the last days of his life he remarked, "I die now, loving my friends, not hating my enemies, adoring God and detesting superstition." Fear of death had shifted in his experience so that the thought of death enriched his life. Like the spirit of the apostle Paul, beautifully framed in the words of Robert Southwell, Voltaire had learned, "Not where I breathe, but where I love, I live." The proper thought of death causes one to die to pride, suspicion, resentment, fear, jealousy; it resurrects one to a life imbued with *agape.* He who learns how to "die daily" will finally find it but natural to meet death with a faith akin to George Matheson's:

> O love that wilt not let me go,
> I rest my weary soul in Thee;
> I give Thee back the life I owe,
> That in Thine ocean depths its flow
> May richer, fuller be.

2. *Man has a rendezvous with death: he also has a rendezvous with life. The thought of death intensifies the urge to live.* The tragic circumstances of war deepen man's thinking about both life and death. Among the poets who sang their phrases about death in World War I, none spoke a higher word than Alan Seeger,

> I have a rendezvous with Death,
> At some disputed barricade,
> When Spring comes back with rustling shade,

I BELIEVE CONTEMPLATION OF DEATH ENRICHES

And apple blossoms fill the air;
I have a rendezvous with Death.
When Spring comes back, blue days and fair.[2]

While this was a poem for war, it also expresses every man's feeling about death in time of peace. Like Alan Seeger, who laid down his pen and kept his rendezvous, so must every man at some time keep a tryst with death. War only emphasizes the immediacy of death. Peacetime is more patient in bringing this experience to most of us. Yet both war and peace challenge man not merely to die but also to live with intensity.

Alan Seeger's graphic words depicted man's rendezvous with death. His idea was echoed by Countee Cullen, then an eighteen-year-old Negro boy, a senior in a New York City high school, who spoke about man's rendezvous with life:

I have a rendezvous with Life,
In days I hope will come,
Ere youth has sped, and strength of mind,
Ere voices sweet grow dumb.
I have a rendezvous with Life,
When Spring's first heralds hum.[3]

Man needs thoughts which will intensify his living, and the thought of this rendezvous with death adds depth and activity to man's rendezvous with life. On a highway not far from my home is a series of religious signs; one of them has this sentence, "Where will you spend eternity?" In the background of the sect which placed this sign on the highway is the thought that such an idea may cause some readers to shift their patterns of contemporary living because of fear of the grave. Perhaps some are affected by such an idea, but most of us are concerned with a type of experience higher than one stimulated by fear of death. This higher motive

[2] "A Rendezvous with Death." By permission of Charles Scribner's Sons.
[3] "A Rendezvous with Life," *Caroling Dusk* (New York: Harper & Bros., 1927). By permission of Harper & Bros.

81

concerns itself with daily intensified living. We may believe in the immortality of the individual, but *this* world is certain and we want a drive for the temporary scene.

Proper thought of death should be constructive; it should urge a person to live his life with every degree of intensity. It should make him realize that he wants to spend each moment richly in order that he may feel heroism and adventure as a part of his total experience. A friend of mine expresses this feel toward life thus:

> Afraid to live? Nay, I would grow,
> Triumph, conquer, fail, forego.[4]

On the tomb of a minister buried a few blocks from my study I recently saw this inscription:

> I preached as never sure to preach again,
> And as a dying man to dying men.

When I asked one of my friends about this minister, a person who had known him well, he told me this story: "Yes, that inscription well describes him. He died in 1886 at the age of twenty-eight years. On his pulpit he kept that quotation; it was the motivation for his living as well as his preaching. He lived every moment with great intensity, as though it might be the last—and also the best—moment of his life."

The creative thought of death drives a person to consider every hour of his experience as a "giant hour." Because he has been given by God the privilege of living, he does not wish to waste such an experience. He wants it to count for something. He wants to live with a sense of "frantic immediacy."

The wise men of the medical profession do not conceal the incurability of a disease from a patient; they discern that knowledge of death aids the patient and his family to plan with wisdom the time remaining to him. This was the case with Grant Wood, the artist, who in going to the hospital

[4] Clyde Tull.

82

consented to an examination only if the doctors would tell him what malady they might find. The doctors kept their promise; they told him that he had an incurable cancerous growth. When he was informed of this malignancy he resigned from the staff of the University of Iowa because he knew he would never leave the hospital bed. The university refused his resignation—one of the most warming experiences he ever had. Until the end Grant Wood courageously and creatively lived in his hospital room; the thought of death intensified the living of his remaining days.

No more glorious story has come out of World War II than the one related of the four chaplains who served on the "Dorchester," a United States transport ship sunk in June, 1943, by a submarine off the coast of Greenland. The chaplains gave their life preservers to four of the combatant men on the boat who were without preservers, since as chaplains they had promised to care for their men in every need. Last reports of these four chaplains—George Fox and Clark Poling, Protestant ministers; Alexander Goode, a Jewish rabbi; and John Washington, a Roman Catholic priest—portrayed them on the sinking ship, arms about one another, singing, "Nearer, my God, to thee!" If in the last few moments before a rendezvous with death men can have such an intensified, courageous rendezvous with life, ought it not to be possible that the whole span of life be lived with a similar intensity? The thought of death does intensify the urge to live if death is seen in its proper perspective.

3. *While men do not agree on the type or degree of immortality in which they believe, all thoughtful men are affected in their present living by whatever belief in immortality they hold.* Several years ago I heard Dr. Edward S. Ames give his *credo*. At one place in his sermon he said, "I believe that man is worthy of long remembrance." This was his view of man's immortality, a remembrance resident in the memories of men and women of future generations. Such an attitude toward immortality is that of the religious

humanist who believes that we may accept only those religious ideas which can be observed by use of the scientific method: man is "immortal" only in so far as he leaves an impression upon his environment (social immortality) or hands his heritage of life to his children and his children's children (biological immortality). If scientific research sometime gives more data of a psychic nature to prove that man is alive as a personality after the grave, then the humanist will believe more about the immortality of the individual person; but until he has scientific data from psychic research, he is agnostic about any type of immortality beyond biological and social influences. While this view of eternal life may not appeal to some people, the thought of his influence resting in a better society after his death drives the humanist to live with deep intensity that he may leave his best contribution in the social scene. Like the "builders" in Longfellow's words the humanist would say:

> Build to-day, then, strong, and sure,
> With a firm and ample base;
> And ascending and secure
> Shall to-morrow find its place.[5]

The thought that tomorrow shall "find its place" in the human structure is sufficient to drive the humanist to noble and unselfish living in the social scene.

The Christian theist agrees with the scientific humanist's view about death's enrichment of life, but theism goes beyond humanism. Differing from the humanist, the theist discerns the conservation of values as not merely in man and society; values of personalities are ultimately conserved in God. Professor Arthur H. Compton, famous physicist, states well the theist's position for believing in personal immortality:

The evolutionary process [on this planet] is working toward the development of conscious persons rather than toward the development of a physical organism. . . . We should not look upon

[5] "The Builders."

84

I BELIEVE CONTEMPLATION OF DEATH ENRICHES

consciousness as the mere servant of the biological organism, but as an end in itself. . . . The thoughts of man . . . are conceivably to the Lord of Creation among the most important things in the world. From this point of view we might expect nature to preserve at all costs the living souls which it has evolved at such labor. This would mean the immortality of the individual consciousness. . . . The exercise and discipline of youth, the struggles and failures and success . . . of maturity, the loneliness and tranquillity of age—these make up the fire through which [man] must pass to bring out the pure gold of his soul. Having thus been perfected, what shall nature do with him? Annihilate him? What infinite waste! [6]

My wife's grandfather was fortified with a Christian theistic faith that death would open up a larger world of adventurous experience for him. His last years in this temporal span were intensely lived with patience, expectancy, peace, humility, courage. During my last visit with him, when he was eighty-five years of age, he said to me, "I can hardly wait until I pass into the larger area of life through the portal of death. What marvelous experiences await me there—so many things there I shall be able to do which thus far I have never had time to accomplish!" The thought of his death beautifully intensified his pattern of living.

Nowhere in the Christian tradition do we find death and life more deeply intertwined than in the thoughts of Paul and John in their New Testament writings. Paul always viewed Christ's death and resurrection as belonging together. Furthermore Christ's death and resurrection had "cosmic" value, somehow mysteriously affecting every Christian believer. Paul explained it thus: Christ had a spiritual body. Paul found his relation to the spiritual Christ via faith at his conversion on the Damascus road. There Paul's old psychic self was crucified, and he was resurrected to a new spiritual self. The Church is the continuing "Body of Christ" for Christians who through faith find their proper relation to God and

* The Freedom of Man, p. 153.

85

man in *agape*. Thus the Easter experience for Paul was not an event to be celebrated on one Sunday each year; it was an experience daily celebrated by those who through faith find their proper relation to God's *agape* and translate this spirit of *agape* within their community. Thus the resurrected life for the Christian is one filled with redemptive love; it is the result of his death to fear, selfishness, a sense of guilt, resentments, and the other evils which lay waste life.

In the Gospel of John the mystical writer says that for the believers—people of faith—"eternal life" is a quality of experience here and now. Such a thought of death sees the grave as merely a moment when each believer graduates from this temporal world into the eternal world. Translating the feeling of the Gospel of John in modern times, Henry H. Saunderson has written:

> In thinking of immortality, we are too much inclined to put first emphasis on length instead of on quality. We seek the assurance that life will be projected on a line that runs into the far future instead of seeking now the higher levels of life, where the assurance of immortality will come unsought. The immortal life has begun, and the eternal world is all about us, waiting to be discovered. Men ask very wistfully if there be another life at the far end of this life; and then Life turns to the questioner and asks him if he dares to live now the life immortal, and offers him the priceless reality as a present attainment. . . . Immortality stands before us with its supreme challenge, saying, "If ye then *be risen* with Christ, seek those things which *are above.*" It asks us this poignant question—"Do you dare to live here and now the life immortal? Are you ready for the adventure of trusting yourself to the tides of the Spirit? Will you live for the sake of the things which cannot perish?" [7]

Paul, John, and other Christian thinkers through the centuries have believed in the preservation of personalities through eternity mainly because they have believed in a Christlike God. Bishop Francis J. McConnell vividly expresses such a view:

[7] W. L. Stidger, ed., *If I Had Only One Sermon to Preach on Immortality* (New York: Harper & Bros., 1929), pp. 313, 317.

I BELIEVE CONTEMPLATION OF DEATH ENRICHES

I leave it all [regarding personal immortality] with the thought of the God revealed in Christ. Assuming such a God, it seems to me that we have to hold fast to human immortality to preserve the Christ-revelation of God. If we have not a God Christlike in moral qualities our reflections about immortality will not be worth much.[8]

And I presume that is where the case rests for most Christians.

4. *The roots of modern man's view of life and death are deeply imbedded in both the Greek and the Hebrew traditions. For both the Greek and the Hebrew the thoughts of death enriched life: Socrates (the father of Greek philosophy) and Jesus (the highest result of the Hebrew tradition) clearly illustrate such a thesis.*

Socrates, as interpreted by Plato in the *Dialogues,* viewed life as a prologue or rehearsal for death. All souls were of divine origin under divine guidance. Before his judges Socrates exclaimed, "Those of us who think that death is an evil are in error. . . . Wherefore, O judges, be of good cheer about death, and know this of a truth—that no evil can happen to a good man, either in life or after death." Shortly before his death Socrates further affirmed, "Fair is the prize, and the hope great! . . . I say, let a man be of good cheer about his soul, . . . who has adorned the soul in her own proper jewels, which are temperance, and justice, and courage, and nobility, and truth—in these arrayed she is ready to go on her journey . . . when her time comes." When Socrates is asked by Crito, "In what way would you have us bury you?" Socrates replies, "In any way that you like; only you must get hold of me, and take care that I do not walk away from you. . . . Be of good cheer, then, my dear Crito, and say that you are burying my body only, and do with that as is usual, and as you think best."

Before Socrates raised the cup of poison to his lips he said, "I may and must pray to the gods to prosper my journey

[8] *Ibid.,* p. 173.

from this to the other world—may this then, which is my prayer, be granted to me." To his friends about him he said, "Be quiet then, and have patience." And then to his friend Crito he spoke his last words, "I owe a cock to Asclepius; will you remember to pay the debt?" Several moments later his friends knew that Socrates had passed from this world to the greater world. Remarks his biographer, "Such was the end of our friend, concerning whom I may truly say, that of all men of his time whom I have known, he was the wisest and the justest and the best." [9] Was not Socrates' view of death —which lent him courage, humility, sympathy, love—one of the basic factors which enriched his view of life?

The way in which Jesus died on a cross seems to leave more of an impression in the minds of his interpreters than the way in which he lived. Paul's gospel centers almost entirely about the crucifixion and the resurrection of Jesus. The Gospel of Mark—copied carefully by the compilers of the Gospel of Matthew and the Gospel of Luke—lends almost one half of its contents to the passion story, beginning where Jesus says to his disciples, "The Son of man must suffer . . . and be killed. . . . Whosoever will come after me, let him deny himself, and take up his cross, and follow me. For whosoever will save his life shall lose it." (Mark 8:31, 34, 35.) Mark then gives one fifth of his Gospel to the last "week" which Jesus spent in Jerusalem. The Epistle to the Hebrews centers its interpretation on the sacrificial death of Jesus. For all of these interpreters the way Christ died seemed to set a seal on the way Christ lived. He who had said, "Whosoever shall lose his life . . . shall save it," "Let him . . . take up his cross, and follow me," "Greater love hath no man than this, that a man lay down his life for his friends," Forgive "seventy times seven," "Thy will be done," seemed to believe what he said; for Jesus on the cross exemplified that his thoughts at this tragic moment of death were the thoughts which he had taught in his intensity of living. On the cross, shortly before

[9] These excerpts are from the *Apology* and the *Phaedo*, Jowett translation.

88

the end, Jesus said of his persecutors, "Forgive them; for they know not what they do." Amid the pain of his crucifixion Jesus was able to utter, "Father, into thy hands I commend my spirit." Within hearing distance of Jesus' last mortal words was a Roman centurion, deeply affected by the way Jesus died. The centurion's words were these, "Truly this man was the Son of God." For had not Jesus through his faith in God and his redemptive attitude toward man shown *agape* in its highest focus?

Yes, I believe that man's Christian thoughts about death enrich his life. Like Jesus we should see life as "lent to be spent," [10] as an adventure in which we can say with Jacopone da Todi that a saint is "one in whom Christ is felt to live again." Surely death has no barriers for a life filled with *agape*. As a Christian theist I believe that God has some plan for the conservation of personalities in the eternal adventure.

[10] Douglas Steere, *On Beginning from Within*, p. 148.